Vinh Liem

Two Faces
Of Life

Essays

Lulu.com
2008

Two Faces of Life
Essays
By **Vinh Liem**

Library of Congress Catalog Card Number:
International Standard Book Number: 978-0-578-00036-7

$15.95 USA / $20.50 CAN

Table of Contents

PART III: SOCIETY, POLITICS, AND RELIGION

Books published in the United States

1. Tị Nạn Trường Ca, Tập I (The Refugee's Lasting Chantey) – Book of poems, Vol. I, written in Vietnamese, published in 1980
2. Bi Ca Người Vượt Biển (Lament of The Boat People) – Book of poems, written in Vietnamese, published in 1980
3. Tị Nạn Trường Ca, Tập II (The Refugee's Lasting Chantey) – Book of poems, Vol. II, written in Vietnamese, published in 1982
4. Gã Tị Nạn (The Refugee Guy) – A collection of short stories, written in Vietnamese, published in 1986
5. Without Beginning Without End – Poetry, English, published in 2008
6. Lament of The Boat People – Poetry & Essays, English & Vietnamese, published in 2008

About the Author

Vinh Liem

Vinh Liem was born in South Vietnam in 1944. He joined the Vietnamese Navy in 1964. After the fall of South Vietnam, he fled his country and eventually settled in the United States in September 1975.

Vinh Liem has been a poet, writer and journalist since 1964 and between 1980 and 1986, he published four books of poems and short stories in the United States. His latest publications were published by Lulu.com in April 2008: Without Beginning Without End (Poetry, in English) and Lament of The Boat People (Poetry & Essays, in English and Vietnamese).

Vinh Liem's poems have also been published by several respected organizations and magazines, including The Vietnam Forum ('Winter-Spring' 1983); the Vietnamese Pen Club Overseas ('War and Exile' 1987); The National Library of Poetry in Owings Mills, Maryland ('A Break In The Clouds' 1993, 'At Day's End' 1994, and 'Divining Beauty' 2001). British publishers, Noble House, published the 'Theatre of the Mind' in 2003. One poem ('Enemy') was recorded in *'The Sound of Poetry'*, released both on compact disk and cassette tape in Fall 2001, by The International Library of Poetry.

Since the fall of South Vietnam in 1975, Vinh Liem has contributed to many Vietnamese newspapers and magazines in the United States, as well as publications in Canada, Europe, Asia, and Australia.

From 1979 to 1981, Vinh Liem was the managing editor of *Hanh Trinh* magazine and the *Hanh Dong* newspaper in Washington, D.C. He has also been the editor-in-chief of *The Vietnam Times* (Washington, D.C.) from 1984 to 1985, and the *Sao Trang* magazine (Miami, FL) from 1992 to 1994.

Address: 1 Applegrath Court, Germantown, MD 20876-5613 (U.S.A.)
Email: vinhliem9@hotmail.com

Community and Organization Activities:

1999 – 2002	Acting Chairman of Association of Free Vietnamese Writers and Artists
1995 – 2001	Coordinator of Democracy for a Free Vietnam
1995	Coordinator, April 30th Commemoration Committee
1994 – 1995	Coordinator of Committee for Defending the National Cause
1993 – 1999	Chairman of Association of Free Vietnamese Writers and Artists
1993 – 1995	Member of The Standing Committee, Vietnamese Community at MD-DC-VA
1992 – 1995	President of Vietnamese ISAW Committee
1989 – 1995	Founder and President of Vietnamese Overseas Experts and Youth Association
1981 – 2001	Founder and President of Viet Club, Inc.
1980 – 1993	Member of Vietnamese Pen Club Overseas
1980 – 1990	Member of Young Republican, Maryland
1980 – 1986	Vice President of Vietnamese Communities Overseas
1976 – 1979	Co-Founder and General Secretary of Vietnamese Community at St. Louis, Missouri

Preface

During my 33 years in the United States, I wrote around two dozen essays in English for my hobbies and my school projects. These essays reflected my view of philosophy, politics, and human rights of the time. Today, I have reviewed them and selected 16 essays for this book – Two Faces of Life. Why did I choose this title? I thought that everybody might have two faces: one for the real person (as same as the front of a medal) and one for the hidden side, where there are secret thoughts and goings-on.

I have divided this book into three parts.

Part I: Literature
1. Pearl's Functions: The Character of Flame in The Scarlet Letter
2. A Comparison Of William Bradford's Writings To Thomas Jefferson's Writings
3. Anne Bradstreet's Poetry In Comparison To Phillis Wheatley's Poetry
4. A Comparison Of John Winthrop's Writings (The Puritan Writer) To Thomas Paine's Writings (The Age Of Reason)
5. A Comparison Of Emerson's "Each and All" To Dickinson's "I heard a Fly buzz – when I died"
6. Two Disenfranchised Writers: Harriet Jacobs and Frederick Douglass

Part II: Biography
1. Rabiah Balkhi: The Medieval Afghani Poet
2. Helen Keller
3. Golda Meir
4. Sam Houston

Part III: Society, Politics, and Religion
1. The Concept of "America" and Being "American" in the 1750's and 1760's
2. Two Basic Differences between Transcendentalism and Anti-transcendentalism
3. The Monroe Doctrine
4. Pirates in The Gulf of Thailand
5. My Motherland
6. Characteristics of Hoa-Hao Buddhism

If you have any suggestions or comments, please let me know. I appreciate your time. You can contact me on vinhliem9@hotmail.com

Good reading!

Vinh Liem

(Germantown, April 30, 2008)

Acknowledgments

I would like to give special thanks to Carlie Lee (London, England), my proofreader, who contributed to this edition.

Germantown, May 26, 2008 (Memorial Day, U.S.)

Vinh Liem

PART I: LITERATURE

Pearl's Functions: The Character of Flame in The Scarlet Letter

(Source: Wikipedia - Title page, first edition of *The Scarlet Letter*, 1850)

THE SCARLET LETTER was a novel. It set in the harsh Puritan community of Boston in the seventeenth century. Nathaniel Hawthorne, author of The Scarlet Letter, is concerned with the tension between the public and the private self. The community publicly disgraced and ostracized Hester Prynne. She drew on her inner strength and certainty of spirit to emerge as the true heroine. Arthur Dimmesdale – Hester's lover and Pearl's father – stood as a classic study of self-division. Trapped by the rules of society, he suppressed his passion and disavowed his lover, Hester, and his daughter, Pearl. The Scarlet Letter was not written as realistic or historically accurate fiction; it was a romance, and a creation of the imagination that disclosed the truth of the human heart.

***

The Author

NATHANIEL HAWTHORNE was born on July 4, 1804 in Salem, Massachusetts. He was a descendant of Puritan ancestors. His father died when he was four years old leaving his family unprovided for and forcing them to move into the house of one of his mother's relatives. Hawthorne began his early studies with Joseph E. Worcester,[1] but he was not particularly fond of school, although he was a voracious reader of Shakespeare, Spencer, and Bunyan. Hawthorne graduated from Bowdoin College in Maine, where he had become friends with Henry Wadsworth Longfellow[2] and Franklin Pierce.[3] After graduating, he returned to where his mother was living in Salem.

---

[1] Joseph Emerson Worcester (1784–1865) was born in August 24, 1784 in Bedford, New Hampshire. After graduating from Yale University in 1811, he taught school in Massachusetts for several years. He was an American lexicographer and chief competitor of Webster's Dictionary in the mid-nineteenth-century. Worcester died on October 27, 1865. He was interred at Mount Auburn Cemetery in Cambridge, Massachusetts.

[2] American poet, educator, and linguist in the nineteenth century (1807-1882).

[3] The Fourteenth President of the United States (1853-1857).

Hawthorne's early endeavors were mostly short stories. He published many tales in magazines and literary annuals. In 1828, Hawthorne published his first novel, *Fanshawe: A Tale*, at his own expense. Then, in 1830, the Salem Gazette published his first story, *The Hollow of the Three Hills*.

In 1837, Hawthorne published his first volume of *Twice-Told Tales*. By 1838, he had written more than two-thirds of the tales and sketches he was to write during his lifetime. Many of them were printed in newspapers, magazines, and the popular literary annuals. In 1842, Hawthorne married Sophia Peabody of Salem. In 1846, Hawthorne published *Mosses from an Old Manse*. His masterpiece, *The Scarlet Letter*, appeared in 1850 and became a national sensation in the United States because of the characters in the novel. Other novels by Hawthorne included *The House of Seven Gables* (1851), *The Blithedale Romance* (1852), and *The Marble Faun* (1860). He died away from home while on a brief vacation with Franklin Pierce in May 1864. Great Britain and the United States proclaimed him the first American romance writer.

The Novel and the Character of Pearl

After twenty-five years of patience, Nathaniel Hawthorne was about to win fame and fortune. He was almost forty-six years old at the time he finished his latest novel – *The Scarlet Letter* – in February 1850. *The Scarlet Letter* sold less than eight thousand copies during Hawthorne's lifetime. He earned only about $1,500. Hawthorne was disappointed in his hope that the sale of the novel would be ten times of that amount.

The cultural context in the novel – *The Scarlet Letter* – represents the function of the New England Puritans as a symbol of national origins. Nathaniel Hawthorne adapted Puritanism in *The Scarlet Letter*. The cultural legacy in *The Scarlet Letter* is a nature of the New England society.

In discussions of *The Scarlet Letter*, there has been a little attention given to the significance of Pearl, the illegitimate daughter of Hester Prynne and Arthur Dimmesdale. The lack of motivation for the confession of Dimmesdale may be seen as a weakness in the plot. According to Anne Marie McNamara, "Since it is obvious that neither Hester nor Chillingworth constitutes an external cause for Dimmesdale's volte face, it seems reasonable to consider the possibility that Pearl may be the agent who effects his unexpected public confession of paternity."[4]

Above all, Pearl is more than a passive link between her mother and her father. She is also more than a static symbol of their sin. She is not merely a fantastically decorative relief in the somber story, but a functional element, a cause of the denouement, and thus provides the motivation for Dimmesdale's final act.

Pearl is a spiritual child. She operates plausibly as an efficient cause within the *ambiance* of ambiguity that pervades the novel. She causes a transformation in the realm of the spirit; the effect is translatable in the terms of the spirit. Above and beyond the literal reality of her action as Hester and Dimmesdale's child, she moves authoritatively as a regenerative influence on the level of *operative* symbol. This is an extraordinary action of an extraordinary child.

(Source: Wikipedia – 1995 film poster)

---

4   Anne Marie McNamara, "The Character of Flame: The Function of Pearl in The Scarlet Letter," On Hawthorne: The Best from American Literature (Durham: Duke University Press, 1990), p. 65.

Through the novel – *The Scarlet Letter* – a family is striving to come into being. Little Pearl, in her innocent wisdom, knows what is needed for them to be whole. Pearl is not merely an ordinary, playful seven-year-old child. She is precociously intelligent, bewilderingly subtle, frighteningly independent, and penetratingly wise. Pearl is a double-nature anomaly. She tortures her mother with misgivings of the nature of her origin. Pearl also exhibits an uncanny curiosity concerning Hester's scarlet letter "A" even in her babyhood. "I wonder," thought Pearl, "if mother will ask me what it means!"[5]

From early childhood, Pearl displays unnatural inquisitiveness about the minister's habit of placing his hand over his heart. She insistently associates these two ostensibly disparate phenomena: curious questioning and implication and prescience. The preternatural endowed child and man are brought together by the author in a cause-effect relationship in the great forest scene.

The double nature of little Pearl's functions has two distinct levels (the natural and the preternatural), two directions (towards a known and unknown parent), and two sets of actions (the explicit and the implicit). It is translatable upon two planes of meaning – the literal and the figurative. Pearl approaches and affects Hester and Dimmesdale in appropriately different ways. On the natural level, Pearl acts on Hester as a real child. On the preternatural level, she acts on Dimmesdale as a "more-than-child," an elf-dryad-nymph child, and a spirit child. "In each case, her method of approach is determined by the nature of the desired effect."[6]

---

5   Nathaniel Hawthorne, "The Scarlet Letter," New York: Penguin Books (1983), p. 155.

6   Anne Marie McNamara, "The Character of Flame: The Function of Pearl in The Scarlet Letter," On Hawthorne: The Best from American Literature (Durham: Duke University Press, 1990), p. 68.

As a real child, Pearl causes a visible change in Hester by audibly, imperiously, and petulantly demanding that Hester should place the discarded A on her breast. Hester understands and obeys Pearl's request. In fact, the estrangement between the mother and child is immediately mended: Pearl leaps the brook and embraces her mother. Furthermore, the estrangement between Pearl and Dimmesdale is not a temporary condition; it is induced by one act and dissipated by another.

The Dimmesdales' offense against Pearl is the deliberate and guilty concealment of parenthood during her whole lifetime. The healing of this serious breach cannot be effected as the other – immediately, visibly, audibly, and objectively. Otherwise, Pearl's spirit communicates its disapproval. That is her way through a silent, indirect, and subjective language. "In the entire scene at the brook side she does not speak to him with her human voice at all. She addresses him indirectly through her persistent rejection of his advance and through actions ostensibly directed towards her mother."[7]

When Hester is restored to Pearl's favor, she entreats Pearl to greet her father and assures her that he loves her, Pearl phrases in two succinct questions the only terms on which the alienation may be terminated: "Doth he love us? Will he go back with us, hand in hand, we three together, into the town?"[8]

---

[7] IBID, p. 69.

[8] Nathaniel Hawthorne, "The Scarlet Letter," New York: Penguin Books (1983), p. 185.

In the public revelation of the real relationship among the three – Hester, Dimmesdale, and Pearl – Pearl is the only means of reconciliation. She ignores her mother's request that she should love the minister. Pearl replies by a question: "And will he always keep his hand over his heart?"[9] She clearly implies that guilt that will plague Dimmesdale even if he succeeds in the plan for escape with Hester and Pearl. Unfortunately, Pearl receives his embrace only at her mother's insistence and immediately bathes her forehead in the brook to wash away all vestiges of his "unwelcome kiss." "Hereupon, Pearl broke away from her mother, and, running to the brook, stooped over it, and bathed her forehead, until the unwelcome kiss was quite washed off, and diffused through a long lapse of the gliding water."[10]

Pearl's actions at the brook side nettle her mother. When Hester is about to call to Pearl to join her and Dimmesdale, Pearl makes a different distance from them. To Hester, Pearl is "not far off." To Dimmesdale, she is "a good way off."[11] Pearl's outburst at the brook side is directed towards her mother and it affects Dimmesdale traumatically. Dimmesdale's "unacknowledged daughter tells him in her wordless language that his acquiescence to Hester's will to escape is a false answer to his problem and is distasteful to her."[12] Fortunately, Pearl will not enter into arrangements that involve a continuance of Dimmesdale's concealment of sin. After all, Dimmesdale leaves the elf at the brook side in a maze.

---

[9]   IBID, p. 185.

[10] IBID, pp. 185-186.

[11] IBID, pp. 177-178.

[12] Anne Marie McNamara, "The Character of Flame: The Function of Pearl in The Scarlet Letter," On Hawthorne: The Best from American Literature (Durham: Duke University Press, 1990), p. 70.

Hester does not know the cause of the change in Dimmesdale, but Dimmesdale knows it: it is Pearl. From the moment of Pearl's dramatic rejection of him in the forest, Dimmesdale has moved in bewilderment and agony at the conflict within him towards this moment when he identifies her as his daughter. That moment reminds him of a question in the morning. Pearl had asked Hester why the minister had kissed her in the forest but he would not recognize her in the town. When the "dreadful witness" of his sin – his scarlet letter – has been exposed, the dying man speaks to himself. Moreover, the effect of Pearl's major gesture in the direct communication with her father in the forest scene is elucidated in Dimmesdale's passionate disclosure. Pearl's effect was against his will – as she is his daughter. The hidden wound of the scarlet letter is on his breast.

The Scarlet Letter is the founding classic of the American heroic tradition. This does not make it a partisan tract. The novel is no more a polemic against individualist democracy than it is a polemic against adultery. The novel's tragic dual plot asserts: a function of conflict and a condition of conflict. By condition Hawthorne means something unchanging, inevitable, as his appeal to Puritanism indicates – our abiding human limitations. The tragedy lies in a changeable, volatile historical condition.

Furthermore, *The Scarlet Letter* suggests that we have been presented with over and again as alternatives – civic versus individualist heroism, the self-governing community versus Emersonian[13] self-reliance and still-astonishingly-effective social ritual. The novel's major contribution is as a cultural document. Remember that the "society as it has always existed" and the cultural specifics through which condition are represented. Otherwise, *The Scarlet Letter* gives a local habitation and a name to the recurrent, unavoidable conflict between individual and society. Hester, Dimmesdale, and Pearl were the victims of the old Puritan society.

***

Throughout the book, Pearl acts as a symbol. She is an obvious symbol of the illicit love affair between Hester and Dimmesdale. As Pearl develops her personality, she symbolizes the kind of passion that accompanied Hester's sin. As she grows older, her actions and questions are matters of increasing torment to Hester. Pearl plays an active role in Hester's punishment.

Naturally, in any society, the child needs a whole family – both parents – and he or she wants a normal family very much. In this case, Pearl is deprived of a normal family because of Hester and Arthur Dimmesdale's adultery. Pearl is a paradox. Pearl only achieves "wholeness" when Dimmesdale acknowledges his paternity. The duality of Pearl, as illustrated in the scene at the brook, can only be reconciled when Dimmesdale tells all of Boston of his sin and the ultimate result. Dimmesdale's status as a beloved minister would have caused a feeling of betrayal amongst the community, the Puritan persecuted men and women alike. Furthermore, "Pearl is the only visible clue that links him to his crime."[14]

---

[13] The spiritual Emerson was known as Emersonian. Ralph Waldo Emerson (1803-1882) was one of America's best known and best loved 19th century figures.

[14] Michael Ragussis, "Family Discourse and Fiction in The Scarlet Letter,"

The Scarlet Letter, therefore, is another one of those references to the title character. The heraldic language seems to make it more "romantic" in the sense it refers to death and aristocracy. On the other hand, one should never forget Hawthorne's intense sense of irony. Putting such a symbol on one's gravestone almost seems like a defiant act of revenge. This act really reaches out to the community from a lonely person who has reclaimed her nobility in suffering and respect through good works. Or perhaps it was put on the stone by the community, not from her wishes, and thus is a sort of an apology. There are too many ideas, emotions, and overtones that are associated with the one symbol to make a final judgment on what it means. In my opinion, the actions of Pearl in the novel resembled a kind of strange child and a kind of demonic girl in her actions. She is a pitiful child rather than a hateful girl.

(Germantown, Fall 1995)

(Source: Wikipedia - Title page, first edition of *The Scarlet Letter*, 1850)

Modern Critical Interpretations: Nathaniel Hawthorne's The Scarlet Letter (New York: Chelsea House Publishers, 1986), p. 65.

William Bradford
(1590 – 1657)

(Source: Wikipedia)

William Bradford was a leader of the separatist settlers of the Plymouth Colony in Massachusetts. He was elected thirty times to be the Governor of the Plymouth Colony. He was the second signer and primary architect of the Mayflower Compact in Provincetown Harbor.

Born: March 19, 1590 in Austerfield, Yorkshire, England
Died: May 9, 1657 in Plymouth, Massachusetts
Spouse: First wife: Dorothy May (1613 – 1620); second wife: Alice Carpenter Southworth (1623)
Children: William, Mercy, and Joseph
Religion: Christianity
Governorship: 1621 – 1633, 1635 – 1636, 1637 – 1638, 1639 – 1644, 1645 – 1657
Book: *Of Plymouth Plantation*

Thomas Jefferson
(1743 – 1826)

(Source: Wikipedia)

Jefferson was a correspondent, statesman, a writer, a historian, and a politician.

Born: April 13, 1743 in Albermarle County, Virginia
Died: July 4, 1826 in Monticello, Virginia
Spouse: Martha Wayles Skelton
Education: College of William and Mary
Political Party: Republican
Political Activities: Congressman (Virginia House), an author of the
    Declaration of Independence, Minister to French (1785),
    Secretary of State, Vice President of the United States, President
    of the United States
Presidency: Third President of the United States (1801 – 1809)

A Comparison Of William Bradford's Writings To Thomas Jefferson's Writings

(Source: Faith.propadeutic.com &Wikipedia)

Despite William Bradford living in the seventeenth century and Thomas Jefferson living in the eighteenth century, both men were instrumental in establishing the local and federal governments, which they later served. William Bradford and Thomas Jefferson had similar ideas about the plantation covenants, the liberty of mind, and the model of life, but they had different ideas about the *purpose* of government. I will discuss both their similar and different ideas.

***

William Bradford was the first governor of Massachusetts. His duties involved different fields of service. He was a chief judge and jury, superintendent of agriculture and trade, and made allotments of land. According to the Norton Anthology, William Bradford's own life provided a model of the life of the community. Bradford and his Mayflower fellows wished to follow Calvin's model[15] and to set up particular churches in the New World. They were known as "Separatists," especially Bradford, who was deeply committed to the Puritan cause.

---

[15] John Calvin (1509-1564) was a French Protestant theologian during the Protestant Reformation and was a central developer of the system of Christian theology called Calvinism or Reformed theology.

Thomas Jefferson was the third president of the United States. He was also the First Secretary of State, Minister to France, and Governor of Virginia. Thomas Jefferson was a Member of Congress and an author of the Declaration of the Independence. He was a writer and a supporter of the Virginia State for Religious Freedom, and a founder of the University of Virginia. Thomas Jefferson was known as an architect and designer of the Virginia state capital. He was known all over the world for his spirit of scientific inquiry. He was also known as the creator of a number of remarkable inventions.

The similarities in their ideas

William Bradford believed in plantation covenants. Those covenants were designed to protect the rights of citizens beyond the reach of established governments. He was a person who enjoyed study as well as action.

On the other hand, Thomas Jefferson also believed in the liberty of the mind and the values of the land. He was always more interested in the practical consequences of ideas.

The differences in their ideas

One of William Bradford's differences in view was in religion. He followed Calvin's model and set up "particular" churches in the New World. William Bradford was deeply committed to the Puritan cause.

(Source: Peter A Levey – Flickr.com – The Plymouth Plantation)

In his book entitled *Of Plymouth Plantation*, Book I, Chapter IX, William Bradford wrote: *"What could now sustain them but the Spirit of God and His Grace? Mat not and ought not the children of these fathers rightly say 'Our fathers were Englishmen which came over this great ocean, and were ready to perish in this wilderness; but they cried unto the Lord, and He heard their voice and looked on their adversity,' etc. 'Let them therefore praise the Lord, because He is good: and His mercies endure forever.' 'Yea, let them which have been redeemed of the Lord, show how He hath delivered them from the hand of the oppressor. When they wandered in the desert wilderness out of the way, and found no city to dwell in, both hungry and thirsty, their soul was overwhelmed in them. Let them confess before the Lord His loving kindness and His wonderful works before the sons of men.'"* [16]

Thomas Jefferson distrusted all rulers and geared the rise of an industrial proletariat. He was an honest aristocrat in manner of life and personal tastes. Thomas Jefferson wished to include a strong statement against slavery. He denied all parliamentary authority over America and argued that ties to the British monarchy were voluntary and not irrevocable. Thomas Jefferson wished to place the British people on record as the Ultimate cause of the Revolution. Furthermore, Thomas Jefferson's lifelong passion liberated the human mind from tyranny. He was the author of the Declaration of the Independence and *"Notes on the State of Virginia."*

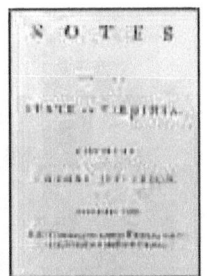

(Source: StateVA.Vahistorical.org)

---

[16] "The Norton Anthology of American Literature," Volume 1. W.W. Norton & Company, New York (1998), p. 177.

Thomas Jefferson believed in the freedom of religion. He wrote: *"The present state of our laws on the subject of religion is this. The convention of May 1776, in their declaration of rights, declared it to be a truth, and a natural right, that the exercise of religion should be free; but when they proceeded to form on that declaration the ordinance of government, instead of taking up every principle declared in the bill of rights, and guarding it by legislative sanction, they passed over that which asserted our religious rights, leaving them as they found them. The same convention, however, when they met as a member of the general assembly in October 1776, repealed all acts of parliament which had rendered criminal the maintaining any opinions in matters of religion, the forbearing to repair to church, and the exercising any mode of worship; and suspended the laws giving salaries to the clergy, which suspension was made perpetual in October 1779."* [17]

* * *

William Bradford was a self-educated person. Historians believed that the crown of all his life was his holy, prayerful, watchful and fruitful walk with God. In contrast, Thomas Jefferson was highly educated in Latin and Greek. He was a politician, but he was not a political thinker. Thomas Jefferson was always "eager after information" and he was determined to improve himself.

(Germantown, Fall 1998)

(Source: uncpress.unc.edu)

---

[17] IBID, p. 727.

Anne Bradstreet
(1612 – 1672)

(Source: Annebradstreet.com)

*Anne Bradstreet was one of the most prominent figures in the
American literature history in the 17th century. She was the first
American poet, a writer, a feminist and a free thinker. Anne
Bradstreet was a Puritan wife who was against the hardships of
New England colonial life. She was also a testament to the plight of
the women of the age. Besides poetry, she wrote about history,
politics, theology, and medicine.*

Born: Anne Dudley in Norhampton, England in 1612
Died: September 16, 1672 in Andover, Massachusetts, at the age 60
Parents: Thomas Dudley (Governor of the Massachusetts Bay
    Colony) and Dorothy Yorke
Spouse: Simon Bradstreet (Governor of the Massachusetts Bay
    Colony)

Children: Dorothy
Collection of poems: *The Tenth Muse Lately Sprung Up in America,*
   by a Gentlewoman of Those Parts (1650), *Several Poems*
   Compiled with Great Variety of Wit and Learning (1678).
Poems: *Upon the Burning of Our House July 10th, 1666,*
   Contemplation, To My Dear and Loving Husband.

Phillis Wheatley
(1753 – 1784)

(Source: Wikipedia - Phillis Wheatley statue
on Commonwealth Ave. in Boston
as part of the Boston Women's Memorial)

Phillis Wheatley was the first published African-American poet. She
was popular as a poet both in the United States and England in the
18th century.

Born: 1753 in Gambia, Africa

Died: December 5, 1784

Slavery: Phillis Wheatley was purchased by John Wheatley, Boston, Massachusetts and she became a slave at the age of seven. She was freed from slavery on October 18, 1773

Education: The Wheatley taught her to read and write English and helped encouraged her poetry

Religion: Christian

Spouse: John Peters

Children: 3

Poems: *On being brought from Africa to America, An Address to the Atheist* (1767), *An Address to the Deist* (1767), *To the King's Most Excellent Majesty* (1768), *Atheism* (1769), *An Elegiac Poem On the Death of that celebrated Divine, and eminent Servant of Jesus Christ, the Reverend and Learned Mr. George Whitefield* (1771), *A Poem of the Death of Charles Eliot* (1772), *To His Honor the Lieutenant Governor on the death of his Lady* (1773), *An Elegy, To Miss Mary Moorhead, On the Death of her Father, The Rev. John Moorhead* (1773), *An Elegy, Sacred to the Memory of the Great Divine, the Reverend and the Learned Dr. Samuel Cooper* (1784)

Books: *Poems on Various Subjects, Religious and Moral* (1773), *To His Excellency George Washington (1776), Memoir and Poems of Phillis Wheatley, a Native African and Slave (1834)*

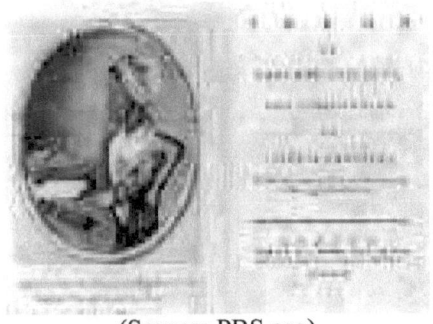

(Source: PBS.org)

Anne Bradstreet's Poetry In Comparison To Phillis Wheatley's Poetry

Poet Anne Bradstreet (1612 – 1672) lived in the seventeenth century. She was an ambitious poet. Her imagination was firmly grounded in English religion, political and cultural history.

Poet Phillis Wheatley (1753 – 1784) was born over a hundred years later than Anne Bradstreet. She was a child prodigy and a former black slave. She challenged the role of slavery as incompatible with Christian life.

In this essay I will discuss the theme, tone, and symbols and imagery that the two poets used in their poems. I will also discuss the place of these two poets in the American literature.

***

Poet Anne Bradstreet was a Puritan. She founded a new world and new manners in this country. On the other hand, Poet Phillis Wheatley was a Christian. She fought to free her people from slavery through literature.

The Theme

Anne Bradstreet's poems reflected her concern for her family and home, and the pleasures she took in everyday life, rather than in the life to come. Her long meditative poems were on the ages of humankind.

In her poem, *The Prologue*, Anne Bradstreet promoted the women's role as well as the equality of men and women in the New World:

> *"Men can do best, and women know it well*
> *Preeminence in all and each is yours;*
> *Yet grant some small acknowledgment of ours."* [18]

Anne Bradstreet's wonderful world was her family, especially her father. In her poem, *To Her Father with Some Verses*, I discovered that her love for her father was forever and she was in charge of her love.

> *"My stock's so small I know not how to pay,*
> *My bond remains in force unto this day;*
> *Yet for part payment take this simple mite,*
> *Where nothing's to be had, kings loose their right.*
> *Such is my debt I may not say forgive,*
> *But as I can, I'll pay it while I live;*
> *Such is my bond, none can discharge but I,*
> *Yet paying is not paid until I die."* [19]

Phillis Wheatley, on the other hand, always wondered about the human sorrow. She described the human sorrows as follows:

> *"I, young in life, by seeing cruel fate*
> *Was snatched from Afric's fancied happy seat:*
> *What pangs excruciating must molest,*
> *What sorrows labor in my parent's breast?"*

Phillis Wheatley was given freedom (in 1773) but she always wished to fight for freedom from slavery for her people. She believed that people would understand her. Her feeling was in and through her heart.

> *Should you, my lord, while you peruse my song,*
> *Wonder from whence my love of Freedom sprung,*
> *Whence flow these wishes for the common good,*
> *By feeling hearts best understood."* [20]

---

[18] "The Norton Anthology of American Literature," Volume 1. W.W. Norton & Company, New York (1998), p. 248.
[19] IBID, p. 261.
[20] IBID, p. 825.

The Tone

As I mentioned earlier, Anne Bradstreet was a Puritan. She was a firm believer in the Puritan experiment in America. Here are Anne Bradstreet's Puritan beliefs about the Nature of God. She believed that God controlled our nature and fate.

> *"By nature trees do not when they are grown,*
> *And plums and apples thoroughly ripe do fall,*
> *And corn and grass are in their season mown,*
> *And time brings down what is both strong and tall.*
> *But plants new set to be eradicate,*
> *And buds new blown to have so short a date,*
> *Is by His hand alone that guides nature and fate."* [21]

According to the title of her first book of poems, *Poems on Various Subjects, Religious and Moral* (1773), Phillis Wheatley's theme was about religious and moral characters. In her poem, *On the Death of the Rev. Mr. George Whitefield*, Phillis Wheatley prayed for Rev. George Whitefield:

> *"That Savior, which his soul did first receive,*
> *The greatest gift that ev'n a God can give,*
> *He freely offered to the numerous throngs,*
> *That on his lips with listening pleasure hung."* [22]

The Use of Symbols or Imagery

Anne Bradstreet's imagination was firmly grounded in English religions, political, and cultural history. Here is her Puritan concept about life.

> *"A price so vast as is unknown*
> *Yet by His gift is made thine own;*
> *There's wealth enough, I need no more,*
> *Farewell, my pelf, farewell my store.*
> *The world no longer let me love,*

---

[21] IBID, p. 276.
[22] IBID, p. 829.

My hope and treasure lies above. " [23]

Phillis Wheatley challenged the role of slavery. Wheatley's concept about human being – not by race, color, or religion – is as follows:
> *"Once I redemption neither sought nor knew.*
> *Some view our sable race with scornful eye.*
> *'Their color is a diabolic dye.'*
> *Remember, Christians, Negroes, black as Cain,*
> *May be refined, and join the angelic train."* [24]

The poet's place in the American literature

Anne Bradstreet's poems were widely read in England and in the New World between 1650 (her first collection of poetry, *The Tenth Muse Lately Sprung Up in America, By a Gentlewoman of Those Parts*, was printed in London in 1650) and 1678 (her second edition, Bradstreet's poems, was published in 1678). Although Anne Bradstreet was known only as a Puritan poet.

Phillis Wheatley was recognized in the first year of her first publication in London (*Poems on Various Subjects, Religious and Moral*, 1773), but "*she has never been better understood than at the present.*" She was recognized by Henry Louis Gates, Jr. as he had argued, "*Wheatley launched two traditions at once – the black American literary tradition and the black woman's literary tradition. It is extraordinary that not just one but also both of these traditions were founded simultaneously by a black woman – certainly an event unique in the history of literature. It is also ironic that this important fact of common, coterminous literary origin seems to have escaped most scholars.*" [25]

***

---

[23] IBID, p. 279.
[24] IBID, p. 825.
[25] IBID, p. 825.

Anne Bradstreet was known as a Puritan poet. She was the first in a long line of American poets who took their consolation not from theology but from wonderful works. Phillis Wheatley, on the other hand, was a poet of the abolition of slavery. Her principle was "Love of Freedom." Finally, I can say that there were two different worlds between two American poets: Anne Bradstreet and Phillis Wheatley. Anne Bradstreet was a Puritan poet, but Phillis Wheatley was a disenfranchised poet.

(Germantown, Fall 1998)

(Source: poetryfoundation.org & umb.edu)

John Winthrop
(1587 – 1649)

(Source: Wikipedia)

John Winthrop was a respected political figure, a leader of a group of English Puritans to the New World, and an author of the concept of American exceptionalism (the wealthy had a holy duty to look after the poor).

Born: January 12, 1587 or 1588 in Edwardstone, Suffolk, England
Died: March 26, 1649 in Massachusetts
Parents: Adam Winthrop (1548 – 1623) and Anne Browne
Education: Trinity College (Cambridge) and Gray's Inn
Professional: Lawyer at the Court of Wards (London)
Spouse: First wife: Mary Forth (1605 – 1615, 6 children), second wife: Thomasine Clopton (1615 – 1616), third wife: Margaret Tyndal (1618 – 1647, 6 children), fourth wife: Martha Rainsborough (1647 – 1649, 1 child)
Children: 13
Religion: Puritan

Governorship: Governor of the Massachusetts Bay Colony (1630 –
1633, 1637 – 1639, 1642 – 1643, 1646 - 1648)
Book: *The Humble Request of His Majesties Loyal Subjects*
(London, 1630)
Work: *A Model of Christian Charity* (old title: *City upon a Hill*)

Thomas Paine
(1737 – 1809)

(Source: Wikipedia)

*Thomas Paine was an English pamphleteer, revolutionary, radical,
classical liberal, intellectual and inventor. He was known as "The
Father of the American Revolution." He was an early advocate of
republicanism and liberalism. He opposed slavery. He favored free
public education and a guaranteed minimum income.*

Born: January 29, 1737 in Thetford, England
Died: June 8, 1809 in New York City, New York (aged 72)
Parents: Joseph Paine and Frances Cocke
Spouse: First wife: Mary Lambert (1759 – 1761) and second wife:
Elizabeth Ollive (1771 – 1774)
Education: Thetford Grammar School
Religion: Quaker
Political Activities: Member of the 1792 National Convention
(French) and the French National Assembly (1792)
Books: *The Case of the Officers of Excise* (1772), *The Age of
Reason* (1793)
Works: *Common Sense* (1776), *The American Crisis* (1776), *Rights
of Man* (1791), *Agrarian Justice* (1795), *Letter to Washington*
(1796)

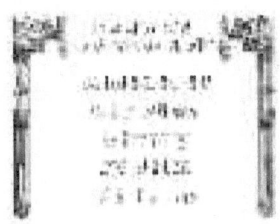

(Source: A Model of Christian Charity-ebookbag.biz &
The Age of Reason-smasharticles.com)

A Comparison Of John Winthrop's Writings
(The Puritan Writer)
To Thomas Paine's Writings
(The Age Of Reason)

John Winthrop was a Puritan writer, but he was not a Separatist. He was "a model of Christian Charity" and a model of the perfect earthly ruler. Winthrop emerged from the story as a person of unquestioned integrity and deep humanity.

On the other hand, Thomas Paine was a writer for the American cause, a writer from "The Age of Reason," and a spokesman for the revolution. He was ridiculed and despised. Thomas Paine's great gift as a stylist was plainness.

In this essay I will discuss a comparison of the writings of both writers.

***

John Winthrop had all the advantages that his father's social and economic position would allow. Winthrop was chosen governor of Massachusetts in 1629. For the next twenty years, most of the responsibility for the colony rested in his hands.

Thomas Paine was a son of a Quaker father and an Anglican mother. He was a corset maker, tobacconist, grocer, schoolteacher, and journalist. Thomas Paine was the anonymous author of *Common Sense*. The purpose of his book was to urge the New World to make its independence immediately from the Great Britain.

The Content

In *A Model of Christian Charity* and *The Journal of John Winthrop*, I found some interesting things about John Winthrop's love of Christianity. These included a viewpoint of laws, the definition of love, the applications of the discourse, the unity of spirit, and the liberty.

A viewpoint of laws – John Winthrop's definition of laws are as follows: *"There is likewise a double law by which we are regulated in our conversation one towards another in both the former respects: the law of nature and the law of grace, or the moral law or the law of the Gospel, to omit the rule of justice as not properly belonging to this purpose otherwise than it may fall into consideration in some particular case."* [26]

The definition of Love – In the Christian view, John Winthrop described his definition of love as follows: *"The definition which the Scripture gives us of love is this: 'Love is the bond of perfection.' First, it is a bond or ligament. Secondly it makes the work perfect."* [27]

The applications of the discourse by the present design – John Winthrop explained his idea as follows: *"It rests now to make some application of this discourse by the present design, which gave the occasion of writing of it. Herein are four things to be propounded: first the person, secondly the work, thirdly the end, fourthly the means."* [28]

(Source: Journal-amb.cult.bg)

---

[26] "The Norton Anthology of American Literature," Volume 1. W.W. Norton & Company, New York (1998), p. 215.

[27] IBID, p. 220.

[28] IBID, p. 223.

The Unity of the Spirit – As John Winthrop explained, *"So shall we keep the unity of the spirit in the bond of peace. The Lord will be our God, and delight to dwell among us as His own people, and will command a blessing upon us in all our ways, so that we shall see much more of His wisdom, power, goodness and truth, than formerly we have been acquainted with."*[29] Fortunately, we must therefore support community and commission. Here are his ideas: *"We must delight in each other, make other's conditions our own, rejoice together, mourn together, labor and suffer together, always having before our eyes our commission and community in the work, our community as members of the same body."* [30]

The Liberty – John Winthrop's ideas about the liberty are as follows: *"For the other point concerning liberty, I observe a great mistake in the country about that. There is a twofold liberty: natural (I mean as our nature is now corrupt), and civil or federal."*

Furthermore, *"This liberty is incompatible and inconsistent with authority, and cannot endure the least restraint of the most just authority. The exercise and maintaining of this liberty makes men grow more evil, and in time to be worse than brute beasts, omnes sumus licentia deteriores."* [31]

In contrast, Thomas Paine's ideas mainly focused on the affairs of the New World as well as Christianity. I will examine some of his ideas.

(Source: Common Sense-americanvision.org)

---

[29]   IBID, p. 225.
[30]   IBID, p. 225.
[31]   IBID, p. 233.

Thoughts on the Present State of American Affairs – In *Common Sense*, Thomas Paine wrote: *"The sun never shined on a cause of greater worth. 'Tis not the affair of a city, a county, a province, or a kingdom; but of a continent – of at least one eight part of the habitable globe. 'Tis not the concern of a day, a year, or an age; posterity is virtually involved in the contest, and will be more or less affected even to the end of time, by the proceedings now. Now is the seed time of continental union, faith and honor. The least fracture now will be like a name engraved with the point of a pin on the tender rind of a young oak; the wound would enlarge with the tree, and posterity read it in full grown characters."* [32]

The American Crisis – In *The Crisis*, the first of sixteen pamphlets, Thomas Paine explained his thoughts of the American crisis as follows: *"These are the times that try men's souls. The summer soldier and the sunshine patriot will, in this crisis, shrink from the service of their country; but he that stands it now, deserves the love and thanks of man and woman."* [33]

Profession of Faith – In *The Age of Reason*, Thomas Paine discussed his faith and his belief in one God. He wrote: *"As several of my colleagues and other of my fellow citizens of France have given me the example of making their voluntary and individual profession of faith, I also will make mine; and I do this with all that sincerity and frankness with which the mind of man communicates with itself."*

"I believe in one God, and no more; and I hope for happiness beyond this life."

"I believe the equality of man, and I believe that religious duties consist in doing justice, loving mercy, and endeavoring to make our fellow creatures happy." [34]

---

[32]   IBID, p. 694.
[33]   IBID, p. 699.
[34]   IBID, p. 706.

Missions and Revelations – Thomas Paine's viewpoint of the mission from God is as follows: *"Every national church or religion has established itself by pretending some special mission from God, communicated to certain individuals."* [35] He also discussed the revelation with God: *"Revelation when applied to religion, means something communicated immediately from God to man."* [36]

The Theology of the Christians – His last idea, but not least, was the Theology of the Christians. Thomas Paine's thought on the theology are as follows: *"As to the Christian system of faith, it appears to me as a species of atheism; a sort of religious denial of God. It professes to believe in a man rather than in God."* Furthermore, he wrote, *"The effect of this obscurity has been that of turning everything upside down, and representing it in reverse; and among the revolutions it has thus magically produced, it has made a revolution in theology."* [37]

He continued, *"As the theology that is now studied in its place, it is the study of human opinions and of human fancies concerning God. It is not a study of God Himself in the works that He has made, but in the works or writings that man has made; and it is not among the least of the mischiefs that the Christian system has done to the world, that it has abandoned the original and reproach, to make room for the hag of superstition."* [38]

(Source: A Model of Christian Charity-ebookbag.biz)

---

[35] IBID, p. 706.
[36] IBID, p. 707.
[37] IBID, p. 708.
[38] IBID, p. 709.

The Style

John Winthrop delivered his sermon, "A Model of Christian Charity," before his departure from England. That was the ideal of a harmonious Christian community. John Winthrop's style was based on his own rules. His rules are as follows: *"There are two rules whereby we are to walk one towards another: justice and mercy. These are always distinguished in their act and in their object, yet may they both concur in the same subject in each respect; as sometimes there may be an occasion of showing mercy to a rich man in some sudden danger of distress, and also doing of mere justice to a poor man in regard of some particular contract, etc."* [39]

Thomas Paine was a writer from the Age of Reason. He was the most persuasive rhetorician. A sermon he heard at the age of eight impressed him with the cruelty inherent in Christianity and made him a rebel forever. His style was "as plain as the alphabet." Somebody called it "plainness." Furthermore, he wrote, *"I offer nothing more than simple facts, plain arguments, and common sense."* [40]

The Purpose

John Winthrop was a Puritan writer. At Cambridge University, Winthrop was exposed to Puritan ideas, but he was not a Separatist. He wished to reform the national church from within, purging it of everything that harked back to Rome, especially the hierarchy of the clergy and all the traditional Catholic rituals.

Thomas Paine was a rebel. In *Common Sense*, Thomas Paine urged the New World to fight for its independence. In *The Crisis*, Thomas Paine shored up the spirits of the Revolutionary soldiers. In *The Age of Reason*, Thomas Paine confirmed his "Profession of Faith."

---

[39] IBID, p. 215.
[40] IBID, p. 693.

The Attitude

John Winthrop realized that he could not antagonize the king by expressing the Puritan cause openly without losing all that he possessed. Cotton Mather once said that Winthrop was a model of the perfect earthly ruler. Winthrop's ideal of a perfectly selfless community was impossible to realize. Furthermore, Winthrop emerged from the story as a person of unquestioned integrity and deep humanity.

Thomas Paine's early years prepared him to be a supporter of the Revolution. He was also an enlisted man in the Revolutionary Army. Thomas Paine was a remarkable, self-taught, and curious person. He opposed slavery. Thomas Paine was also a spokesman for the anti-slavery group in Philadelphia. He was ridiculed and despised. Thomas Paine was too indiscreet and hot tempered for public employment. He received a number of political appointments as rewards for his services as a writer for the American cause, but he did not keep his privileges.

***

John Winthrop was the chosen governor of Massachusetts for twenty years. He emerged "from the story as a person of unquestioned integrity and deep humanity." As Cotton Mather wrote in his history of New England, he chose Winthrop as his "model of the perfect earthly ruler."

Benjamin Franklin once recommended Thomas Paine as an "ingenious, worthy young man." Historians also said that: *"Paine was obviously the right man in the right place at the right time."* But the discrepancy between his high intelligence and the limitations imposed on him by poverty and caste made him long for a new social order. In the last years of his life, Thomas Paine was unhappy and a poor man.

(Germantown, Fall 1998)

Ralph Waldo Emerson
(1803 – 1882)

(Source: Wikipedia)

Ralph Waldo Emerson was a famous American poet in the 19th century. He was an essayist, a philosopher, an orator and a lecturer. He was also known as a transcendental poet. He was a founder of Transcendentalism. He supported the abolitionism.

Born: May 25, 1803 in Boston, Massachusetts
Died: April 27, 1882 (aged 78) in Concord, Massachusetts
Parents: Rev. William Emerson (1769-1811) and Ruth Haskins
    (1768-1853)
Education: Boston Latin School (1812 – 1817), Harvard College
    (1817 – 1821), and Harvard Divinity School
Professional: Schoolmaster (1821 – 1825), Pastor of Boston's

Second Church (1829 – 1829), Unitarian Minister (1829 – 1832)

Spouse: First wife: Ellen Louisa Tucker of New Hampshire (1829 – 1831), second wife: Linda ("Lydian") Jackson of Plymouth (1835 – 1882)

Children (with second wife): Waldo (1836-1842), Ellen (1839-1909), Edith (1841-1929) and Edward (1844-1930)

Religion: Christian

Books: *Nature* (1836), *Essays* (1841), *Essays: Second Series* (1844), *Poems* (1847), *Representative Men* (1850), *English Traits* (1856), *The Conduct of Life* (1860), *May-Day and Other Pieces* (1867), *Society and Solitude* (1870), *Parnassus* (1874), *Letters and Social Aims* (1875)

Works: *The American Scholar* (1837), *Divinity School Address* (1838), *The Dial* (1840-44), *The Poet* (1842), *Experience* (1842), *Each and All* (1847), *Natural History of Intellect* (1870)

Emily Elizabeth Dickinson
(1830 – 1886)

(Source: Wikipedia)

Emily Dickinson was a famous American poet and was regard as an anti-transcendental poet. She was a member of Anti-transcendentalism.

Born: December 10, 1830 in Amherst, Massachusetts
Died: May 15, 1886 by a stroke (aged 55)
Parents: Edward Dickinson and Emily Norcross
Education: Amherst Academy (1840-1846) and Mary Lyon's Mount Holyoke Female Seminary (later became Mount Holyoke College)
Religion: Baptist
Books: *Poems by Emily Dickinson* (First edition, 1890), Poems by *Emily Dickinson* (Second Series, 1891), *Poems by Emily Dickinson* (Third Series, 1896), *Letters of Emily Dickinson* (1894)
Works: Over 1775 poems, including *I heard a Fly buzz – when I died* (1862)

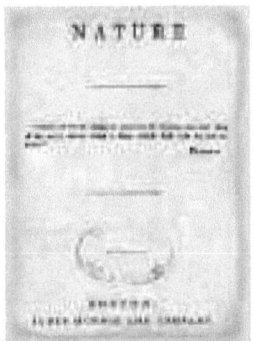 

(Source: Nature-pbs.org & Dickinson-wiredforbooks.org)

A Comparison Of Emerson's "Each and All"
To Dickinson's
"I heard a Fly buzz – when I died"

Ralph Waldo Emerson and Emily Dickinson both lived in the nineteenth century. Emerson was a founder of Transcendentalism and Dickinson was a member of Anti-transcendentalism. Both were famous American poets. Emerson was known as a transcendental poet and Dickinson was regard as an anti-transcendental poet. One of Emerson's famous poems was *"Each and All."* On the another hand, one of Dickinson's famous poems was *"I heard a Fly buzz – when I died."* These two poems have different messages and poetic styles.

In this essay I will discuss both their different messages and poetic styles.

***

Before discussing their poems, I would look over their lives, society, philosophy, and writing.

RALPH WALDO EMERSON was born in Boston on May 25, 1803. He was a son of a Unitarian minister and the second of five surviving boys. His father died when he was eight years old. His father's death left the family to the meager charity of the church. Emerson grew up in the city. At nine years old he was sent to the Boston Public Latin School. Emerson spent 4 years (1817-1821) at Harvard College. After graduation he served as a schoolmaster. He studied theology in 1825 and began preaching in 1826. In 1829 he was ordained as a junior pastor of Boston's Second Church.

Emerson was gradually developing a faith greater in individual moral sentimental than in revealed religion. Emerson married Ellen Tucker of New Hampshire. She died sixteen months later of tuberculosis. In 1832 Emerson notified his church that he had become so skeptical of the validity of the Lord's Supper that he could no longer administer it. A few months later he resigned and embarked on a leisurely European tour. In 1834, he drifted into a quite retreat at Concord, Massachusetts. He continued to preach occasionally and began lecturing at New England lyceums, the public halls that brought a variety of speakers and performers both to the cities and to smaller towns. By this year Emerson came to maturity as a poet. [41]

In 1835 Emerson married Lydia Jackson of Plymouth. His first little book, *Nature* (1836), did not establish him as an important American writer, but it did confirm his future as a prose writer. As the reviewers understood, *Nature* was not a Christian book but one influenced by a range of idealistic philosophies, ancient and very modern. Transcendentalism was being merely the latest name for an old way of thinking. Emerson's immediate reward was having the book become the unofficial manifesto for "the Symposium" of his like-mined friends, which held its first meeting only a few days after *Nature* was published. This group became known as the Transcendental Club. Among the members were the educator Bronson Alcott, the abolitionist and Unitarian minister Theodore Parker, and the Unitarian minister Orestes A. Brownson.

In the early 1830's, death broke up the close-knit band of Emerson brothers. Emerson himself had gone to the south to recover from tuberculosis in 1826-1827. His unsigned contributions to the Transcendentalist's magazine *The Dial* did not enhance his reputation; indeed, he was sometimes attacked in newspapers as the author of Alcott's *Orphic Sayings*, which jocular contemporaries took as the ultimate of transcendental gibberish. Only with the publication of *Essays* (1841) did Emerson's lasting reputation begin.

---

[41] Richardson Jr., Robert D.: Emerson: The Mind On Fire. Berkeley: University of California Press, 1995, p. 176.

By the early 1840s, Emerson's life had settled into its enduring routine. He gave intermittent lectures in Boston and made lecture tours in the Northeast and, later, in the Middle Atlantic States.

After the death of his first son, Waldo, he devoted himself more and more to the personal problems of his circle of family and friends. In 1844 Emerson published *Essays: Second Series*. In *The Poet* he spoke from practical experience as well as theoretical speculation in defining the present state of literature in America. In *Experience* and other essays he resolutely and realistically faced the conflict between idealism and ordinary life.

Emerson slowly gained recognition for his poems, which he collected at the end of 1846. A second trip to Europe (1847-1848) capped his secure middle age. *"Each and All"* [42] was written in this time. As his reputation expanded, he widened his lecture tours into the Midwest. His newest books, among them *Representative Men* (1849) and *Conduct of Life* (1860), were less forceful than his earlier ones.

After long resisting attempts by reformers to gain his support for various social issues, Emerson became a fervent advocate in the 1850s for abolitionism. His efforts, although, were too late and too local to make him a national leader. The rest of Emerson's writing, like the rest of his life, was a slow anticlimax to the intellectual ferment of the years between the mid-1830s and the mid-1840s.

(Source: Virginia.edu)

---

[42] See the poem "Each and All" on page 43.

EMILY ELIZABETH DICKINSON was born on December 10, 1830, in Amherst, Massachusetts. She was the second child of Edward and Emily Norcross Dickinson. Her closet friends were her brother, William Austin, and her sister, Lavinia ("Vinnie"). Neither Emily nor Lavinia married. Emily seldom left Amherst. She attended Amherst Academy from 1840 through 1846. Dickinson's triumph over religious fears was intricately involved in her seeing herself as a poet.

By the early 1860s Dickinson loved Reverend Charles Wadsworth of Philadelphia. She recognized a kindred spirit in the independent, nature-loving man who delighted in being the village crank of Concord. Dickinson's deepest literature debts were to the Bible and to British writers. No one has persuasively traced the precise stages of Dickinson's growth from a conventional schoolgirl versifier to one of the greatest American poets. From her twenties until her death, Dickinson was free to devote much of her life to poetry. She died on May 15, 1886 of a stroke.

The Message

In poetry, each poet did send a message to the reader in his or her poem. In Emerson's *"Each and All"* and Dickinson's *"I heard a Fly buzz – when I died."* [43] I found the message interesting, which represents his and her philosophy of *nature*.

Ralph Waldo Emerson – The *"Each and All"* poem was written in 1847. At this time, Emerson traveled in Europe. This poem is Emerson's concept of <u>nature</u>. "Each" means "individual" or a "self-reliant" and "All" means "the whole." This poem is also Emerson's philosophy. He believes that there is a connection between nature and man. He also confirmed that man is in God and God is inside a man. *"Each and All"* was also the Transcendentalism. "Each" is a basic goodness of an individual in the whole ("All").

---

[43]   See the poem "I heard a Fly buzz – when I died" on page 45.

Emily Dickinson – *"I heard a Fly buzz – when I died"* was written in 1862, the period of time that Emily Dickinson wrote most of her greatest poetry. In the same year, Dickinson wrote to Thomas Wentworth Higginson, editor of *Atlantic Monthly*, to ask him whether her poems were alive. What happened to Emily Dickinson at that time? How it caused her to write this sad poem? What did she mean? What could have account for such behavior in a woman who had been a witty and energetic girl?

Biographers of Dickinson assumed that she had fallen hopelessly in love with a man whose identity has never been established a glamorous but married clergyman. Her man was Reverend Charles Wadsworth of Philadelphia. She met him during her stay in Philadelphia with her sister, "Vinnie," in 1855. There is no evidence that any declaration of love passed between them. Emily had perhaps spoken to him, built of their tenuous relationship an immortal monument to a love that grew out of renunciation. That is a love whose fulfillment lay in unfulfilled. In this poem, Emily sent a message to her lover, Reverend Wadsworth, that she could not love him only when the top of her casket was closed, and she could not see him.

The Poetic Style

Each poet had his or her own style. I have learned that Emerson's poetic style was totally different from Dickinson's poetic style.

Ralph Waldo Emerson's poetic style is strong, clear, and hopeful. **Emily Dickinson**'s poetic style is dismal, dreary, sadly, mournful, doleful, melancholy, lonely, and darksome.

*** *

Ralph Waldo Emerson was a transcendentalist. He believed in nature, social reform, and optimism. On the other hand, Emily Dickinson was an anti-transcendentalist. She was withdrawn from the real world. She brought wit and gaiety to bear upon her tragic sense of life.

(Germantown, Fall 1997)

Each and All

Little thinks, in the field, yon red-cloaked clown,
Of thee, from the hill-top looking down;
And the heifer, that lows in the upland farm,
Far-heard, lows not thine ear to charm;
The sexton tolling the bell at noon,
Dreams not that great Napoleon
Stops his horse, and lists with delight,
Whilst his files sweep round yon Alpine height;
Nor knowest thou what argument
Thy life to thy neighbor's creed has lent:
All are needed by each one,
Nothing is fair or good alone.

I thought the sparrow's note from heaven,
Singing at dawn on the alder bough;
I brought him home in his nest at even;—
He sings the song, but it pleases not now;
For I did not bring home the river and sky;
He sang to my ear; they sang to my eye.

The delicate shells lay on the shore;
The bubbles of the latest wave
Fresh pearls to their enamel gave;

And the bellowing of the savage sea
Greeted their safe escape to me;
I wiped away the weeds and foam,
And fetched my sea-born treasures home;
But the poor, unsightly, noisome things
Had left their beauty on the shore
With the sun, and the sand, and the wild uproar.

The lover watched his graceful maid
As 'mid the virgin train she strayed,
Nor knew her beauty's best attire
Was woven still by the snow-white quire;
At last she came to his hermitage,
Like the bird from the woodlands to the cage,—
The gay enchantment was undone,
A gentle wife, but fairy none.

Then I said, "I covet Truth;
Beauty is unripe childhood's cheat,—
I leave it behind with the games of youth."
As I spoke, beneath my feet
The ground-pine curled its pretty wreath,
Running over the club-moss burrs;
I inhaled the violet's breath;
Around me stood the oaks and firs;
Pine cones and acorns lay on the ground;
Above me soared the eternal sky,
Full of light and deity;
Again I saw, again I heard,
The rolling river, the morning bird;—
Beauty through my senses stole,
I yielded myself to the perfect whole.

Ralph Waldo Emerson

I heard a Fly buzz – when I died

I heard a Fly buzz–when I died–
The Stillness in the Room
Was like the Stillness in the Air–
Between the Heaves of Storm–

The Eyes around–had wrung them dry–
And Breaths were gathering firm
For that last Onset–when the King
Be witnessed–in the Room–

I willed my Keepsakes–Signed away
What portion of me be
Assignable–and then it was
There interposed a Fly–

With Blue–uncertain stumbling Buzz–
Between the light–and me–
And then the Windows failed–and then
I could not see to see–

Emily Dickinson

HARRIET ANN JACOBS
(1813 – 1897)

(Source: Wikipedia)

Harriet Ann Jacobs was a famous abolitionist and writer in the nineteenth century. Her works contributed into American literature and the anti-slavery era.

Born: 1813 in Edenton, North Carolina
Died: March 7, 1897 in Washington, D.C.
Parents: Daniel Jacobs and Delilah (last name unknown)
Slavery: Harriet was born to a slave (owned by John Horniblow). In 1825, Harriet was transferred to the Norcom family. In 1835, Harriet escaped and lived in her grandmother's attic for seven years and later moved to New York City in 1842.
Marriage: Samuel Sawyer (first lover)
Children: Joseph and Louisa (with Sawyer)
Employment: Nursemaid (New York City)

Book: *Incidents in the Life of a Slave Girl* (1861) under the pseudonym Linda Brent

Frederick Douglass
(1818 – 1895)

(Source: Wikipedia)

Frederick Douglass was an American abolitionist, orator, lecturer, author, editor, statesman and reformer. Douglass was one of the most prominent figures in African American history. His real name was Frederick Augustus Washington Bailey.

Born: February 1818 in Talbot County, Maryland
Died: February 20, 1895 (aged 77) in Washington, D.C.
Parents: Aaron Anthony and Harriet Bailey
Slavery: Frederick was born a slave. He was separated from his mother, Harriet Bailey, when he was an infant (about six years old).

Occupation: Antislavery lecturer

Books: *Narrative of the Life of Frederick Douglass, an American Slave* (1845)

His journalistic endeavors: *North Star, Frederick Douglass Weekly, Frederick Douglass' Paper, Douglass' Monthly,* and the *New National Era.*

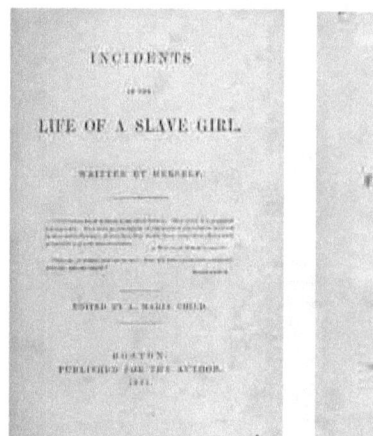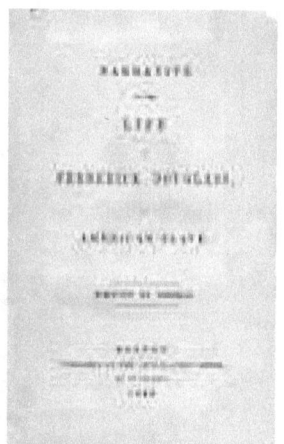

(Source: Wikipedia - Incidents in the Life of a Slave Girl & Narrative of the Life of Frederick Douglass)

Two Disenfranchised Writers: Harriet Jacobs and Frederick Douglass

HARRIET ANN JACOBS and FREDERICK DOUGLASS were born into slavery. They were both famous abolitionists and writers in the nineteenth century. Their works contributed into American literature and the anti-slavery era.

Harriet Jacobs – Harriet Jacobs, also known as Linda Brent, was a slave and narrator. In her autobiography, *Incidents in the Life of a Slave Girl*, author Harriet Jacobs created characters to represent herself and all the historical persons in her life. "Linda Brent" is a pseudonym for the author. Harriet was born into slavery on 1813 in Edenton, North Carolina. She loses both parents at an early age. In her autobiography, Harriet chronicles her early life and her escape from slavery.

Frederick Douglass – Frederick Bailey is Frederick Douglass' real name. Frederick was born in February 1818 in Talbot County, Maryland. He inherited his slave status from his mother, Harriet Bailey, although it was rumored that Frederick's father was white. This rumor does not affect Frederick's social standing as slavery was matrilineal.

***

Their contributions to American literature

Harriet Jacobs
Incidents in the Life of a Slave Girl was long believed to be a fictional account of slavery. It is considered one of the most important antebellum slave narratives. *Incident in the Life of a Slave Girl*, like other narratives, was written as testimony on behalf of and as documentation for the antislavery cause. As such, it represents a highly activist literature, one in which the express purpose was political. Harriet Jacobs participated in the abolitionist movement and was assisted in her literary efforts by other abolitionists.

(Source: Wikipedia)

Incidents in the Life of a Slave Girl offers a critique of slavery rooted in female experience. In addition to exposing the vulnerability of female slaves to sexual exploitation, Jacobs focuses on her roles as a mother, grand daughter, and seeker-of-home. She develops her attack on slavery from within an intricate network of family relations. In the broader context of African-American experience of slavery, children and family become symbols and actual expressions of liberation and freedom. According to Valerie Smith in Introduction: "Jacobs's *Incidents* (writer under the pseudonym of Linda Brent) provides a unique perspective on the complex position of the black woman as slave and as writer." [44]

Like many other slave narratives, *Incidents in the Life of a Slave Girl* is infused with religious reference and poses a scriptural challenge to slavery. The role of religion in slave communities and in African-American history is complex. Harriet Jacobs constructs her story within an explicitly religious framework. Her own religious views show some interesting internal conflicts.

Unlike some authors of slave narratives, Harriet Jacobs does not dwell on her efforts to acquire literacy. The importance of her own literacy is expressed in two ways: Her ability to read the Bible and her literature allows her to write her autobiography.

Frederick Douglass

In 1841, three years after Frederick Douglas escaped from slavery, he launched his career as an abolitionist. In Nantucket, Massachusetts, he spoke for the first time about his slave experiences before a white audience. Before that, he had told his story only to black gatherings. His account was so impressive that the Massachusetts Anti-Slavery Society hired him as a full-time antislavery lecturer.

---

[44] Harriet Jacobs: Incidents in the Life of a Slave Girl. Oxford: Oxford University Press, 1988, p. xxvii.

By 1844, the society was becoming increasingly disturbed, and many doubted Douglass' authenticity. The leaders of the Anti-Slavery Society, therefore, urged Douglass to write his story. The *Narrative of the Life of Frederick Douglass: An American Slave*, including a preface by William Lloyd Garrison and a letter from Wendell Phillips, was published in 1845. Its success was immediate. Thousands of copies were sold both in the United States and in Great Britain. The *Narrative* was even translated into French and Dutch. In short, "*Narrative of the Life of Frederick Douglass* (1845) is the brief, pungent declaration of freedom of a runaway slave writing a powerful antislavery tract." [45]

The ex-slave's story exists in three revised versions: *My Bondage and My Freedom* (1855) – reflections on slavery – and two separate editions of *Life and Times of Frederick Douglass* (1881, 1892) – a memoir. The original version, however, has received the most critical acclaim. The 1845 edition has been praised for its narrative skills, succinctness, and clarity.

Although the *Narrative* is Douglass' masterpiece, he was also a publisher and journalist. He launched this career after returning from England, where he had fled upon the publication of the *Narrative* to avoid being returned to slavery. His journalistic endeavors included the *North Star*, *Frederick Douglass Weekly*, *Frederick Douglass' Paper*, *Douglass' Monthly*, and the *New National Era*.

Their positions in American literature

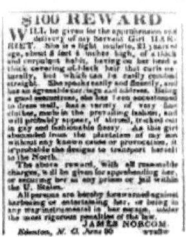

---

[45] McFeely, William S.: Frederick Douglass. London: W. W. Norton & Company, 1991, p. 7.

Harriet Jacobs

Jacobs' autobiography stands among thousands of other written and oral slave testimonies and shares with many of them the themes of bondage, suffering, self-definition, self-assertion, and escape to freedom. Jacobs continued abolitionist efforts during the Civil War and wrote occasionally for the abolitionist press. Jacobs speaks her own life in her own voice. In her autobiography, Jacobs takes the subjective stance of a black woman defining her own experience from a viewpoint deeply rooted in the black slave community. In doing so, she poses a sophisticated and fundamental challenge to white slaveholding American culture. She was the most famous African-American women's writer in the nineteenth century.

Frederick Douglass

Douglass's *Narrative* speaks as eloquently to blacks as it does to whites. Ultimately, the autobiography looks at a timeless theme – man's inhumanity to man – through the lens of slavery. Historically, the *Narrative* is a significant document in the pre-Civil War abolitionist movement. In fact, the last sentence of the appendix reminds the reader of the "sacred cause" for which the autobiography was written. Douglass hopes that his story will hasten the end of "the peculiar institution."

Douglass' *Narrative* belongs to the genre of slave narratives, a popular literary mode from the end of the eighteenth century to the beginning of the Civil War. Thousands of narratives were written during this period, and many were translated into several languages. Douglass' story epitomizes the best of the genre.

Despite his prolific journalist output, Douglass' fame as a writer rests on the *Narrative*. It is a work that will continue to fascinate both historians and literary critics.

***

Harriet Jacobs and Frederick Douglass' narratives and activities contributed to the anti-slavery era and American literature in the nineteenth century. Their contributions were the sources and the inspiration for the anti-slavery activities of black people in the nineteenth and twentieth century.

(Germantown, Spring 1998)

(Source: Wikipedia-Frederick Douglass)

PART II: BIOGRAPHY

Rabiah Balkhi: The Medieval Afghani Poet

The glories of this world and more,
without him are as little;
But Hell, if he were with me,
I should willingly embrace.

Rabiah Balkhi was the pioneer of mystic poetry in the Persian language (Dari) and one of the most outstanding Afghan poets.[46] Her greatest literary contributions were made as the Samanid supremacy (A.D. 890-939) was ending and the Ghaznavid era was beginning (A.D. 989-1149) – the fourth century of the solar calendar.[47] The Ghaznavid era was a golden era of accomplishment for Afghanistan both as empire and as a center of learning and culture. The story of Rabiah Balkhi's life during this time has been told down through the generations.

Childhood

Over one thousand years ago in the city of Balkh, often called the "Mother of cities," a beautiful princess was born in ca. A.D. 1100 in the palace of Kab Quzdari Balkhi – the king of Balkh. From the time of her birth, this little girl was so gentle of manner and so beautiful that her family knew she would be a special joy and pride to them. They named her Rabiah. Many of the people of the kingdom feared that God would claim Rabiah while she was very young because she was reputed to be too beautiful and gentle to live among mortals.

---

[46] Zhobal, Mohammed H. *Tarikh-i Adabyat-i Dari dar Afghanistan*. Kabul: Ministry of Education Printing House, 1956, p. 82.

[47] Rypka, Jan. *History of Iranian Literature*. Dordrecht: D. Reidel, 1968, p. 144.

Rabiah had one brother – Haris, who was a handsome youngster but not of gentle nature. He was very impressed with his own importance as a prince and was rude and unkind to people. He was also intensely jealous of Rabiah because of the attention and love bestowed on her by everyone.

Kab Quzdari Balkhi was a righteous and good king. He encouraged artists, poets, musicians, writers, and athletes to perform in his court. Balkh became a center of learning and culture. Rabiah and her brother often watched these performances. When the performers were finished, the king presented each with a gift for their contributions – and sometimes the king asked Rabiah to make these presentations – which thrilled her and pleased the recipients.

When Rabiah was about ten years old, her mother died. This sorrow led to a closer bond between father and daughter. Raenah, her childhood nurse, now became her constant companion and closest confidant. Rabiah and Raenah spent long hours in the mosque praying and listening to readings from the holy Koran.[48]

Womanhood

As she grew, Rabiah became more beautiful and articulate and developed skills in archery, horsemanship, swimming, and hunting.[49] To celebrate her flowering into womanhood, the king built a suite of rooms especially for her and Raenah. Rabiah began to spend a part of each day writing love poetry – mostly to God. A very religious young woman, she chose this manner to express her love for God. Most of these writings were placed in a locked chest.

---

[48] Nawabi, G. H. *Rabia-i Balkhi*. Kabul: Government Printing House, 1965, p. vii.

[49] Fernea, Elizabeth Warnock and Bezirgan, Basima Qattan. *Middle Eastern Muslim Women Speak*. University of Texas Press, 1984, p. 78.

Haris continued to be jealous of Rabiah's abilities. He insisted that she should be more retiring as a woman and that it was demeaning for a princess to occupy herself writing and reciting poetry.[50]

Among the talented people who appeared at the court were many athletes. One of the greatest was a young slave owned by Haris, named Baktash, who consistently won over all his adversaries. Rabiah often watched these feats of strength and grew to admire the young slave's talents.[51] But she was aware of her position and the responsibilities demanded of her, and she told no one of her admiration for Baktash – not even Raenah. She thought constantly of Baktash and would write down her thoughts in poem form, then lock the poems in her writing chest.[52]

The turning point of life

King Kab Quzdari Balkhi, aged and worn with years of the responsibility of ruling, took to his bed in illness. Haris, impatient to assume the kingship, conspired to hurry his father's death by poisoning him. He decreed that the king was much too ill to see anyone. But Rabiah learned of her brother's plan. She went to her father's bedchamber to warn him. Before she could speak, Haris entered. The king then turned to Haris and informed him that he would be a guest in this palace for only a short time. He admonished Haris to assume the responsibilities of the kingdom and his subjects with honor and righteousness. He gave Rabiah's welfare and happiness into the hands of his son and then quietly slipped away on the arm of death.

---

[50] Nawabi, G. H. *Rabia-i Balkhi*. Kabul: Government Printing House, 1965, p. vii.

[51] Zhobal, Mohammed H. *Tarikh-i Adabyat-i Dari dar Afghanistan*. Kabul: Ministry of Education Printing House, 1956, pp. 82-83.

[52] IBID, p. 83.

With Haris' ascension to the throne, many things in the kingdom changed. Haris was not the wise and righteous ruler that his father had been. Rabiah was more confined to her quarters and allowed less and less to participate in the activities that made her happy. She became ill and restless and spent more of her time writing poetry. Haris was secretly very pleased that Rabiah was ill and hired Sarbatah, an herbal doctor, to mix a concoction of herbs and roots that would cause Rabiah's death. When Sarbatah came to Rabiah's quarters, she refused the medication, explaining that no medicine could cure her illness.

Raenah had become most concerned for Rabiah's health and finally persuaded her to confide in her. Rabiah confessed to Raenah her love for Baktash and the impossibility of ever telling him of this admiration – for she was a princess and he a slave.[53] Raenah was very sad but told Rabiah that if she should need any help in the matter she would do whatever Rabiah wished.

After a time, Rabiah decided to write a poem directly to Baktash. Raenah delivered the poem and Baktash was overwhelmed with the idea that anyone so lovely and gentle as Rabiah should admire him. On his way to see Rabiah, the guards of her suite attempted to stop him, but he overpowered them. After this first meeting, they met several more times and Baktash told Rabiah of his own admiration of her beauty and gentleness.

One day Rabiah found out that her writing chest had been stolen – apparently by someone who thought that it contained her jewels. When the chest was opened and the poems read, there was the name of Baktash, the slave. The chest and its contents were taken to Haris, who immediately assigned Baktash to a post far from the city of Balkh.

---

[53] Nawabi, G. H. *Rabia-i Balkhi*. Kabul: Government Printing House, 1965, p. xix.

Haris's reputation as an unfit king spread far and wide. Finally it reached the ears of one of his oldest and strongest enemies, who sent word that he was on his way to Balkh to challenge Haris in a feat of strength.

Haris was not athletic and knew that he would be no match for his archenemy. In a desperate move, he sent word to Baktash. If Baktash would return to the city of Balkh and defend the honor of its king and the city, he would be rewarded with an influential position and with riches. Baktash returned.

On the day of the contest, Rabiah heard that her brother had ordered the guards to kill Baktash if he should be successful in defeating his adversary. Baktash defended his king well. While the specters in the arena were still cheering Baktash's victory, Rabiah rode a swift steed onto the field of combat, assisted Baktash into the saddle, and rode away – thus saving his life.[54]

The final life

One day Haris received an invitation from the kingdom of Bokhara (now in Russia) to attend a great festival. All the finest artists, writers, poets, musicians, and athletes would gather to compete. Among those presents was one of the greatest writers of the times, Rudaki. He had challenged Rabiah in poetic debate and admired her talent and wisdom. He mentioned her name at the public festival, bemoaning the fact that, despite her poetic talent, gentle ways, and fine upbringing, her heart belonged to Baktash – one of Haris's slaves. Haris became angry. He felt that his own prestige and that of his kingdom had been sorely damaged by the insinuations of Rudaki. He chose to hide his anger in the presence of those at the festival, but as soon as possible he made great haste to return to Balkh. The closer he came to his palace, the more his anger welled within him. He decided that the only possible solution to the intolerable situation was to kill Baktash and Rabiah.

---

[54] IBID, p. xix.

He had Rabiah taken to a public bath where her veins were slashed, and she was left to bleed to death. Raenah helped Baktash escape from the pit and gave him a dagger. Baktash set out for the palace and killed the wicked Haris. He then rushed to the public bath to save the life of his beloved Rabiah – only to find that the warmth of her body was already gone.[55]

Before she died, Rabiah had dipped her finger in her life's blood and written on the walls of the bath the name of Baktash, a poem, and a statement. It told how wrong were her brother's evil thoughts about her love for Baktash (see the excerpts on pages 60-61). Baktash was so despondent over finding Rabiah dead that he too dipped his finger in her blood, wrote her name beside his own, and then fell upon his dagger in death.

Thus ended the life and rule of Haris, which historians have recorded with dishonor – and thus ended the lives of two beautiful, honorable, and talented young lovers. The predictions made by the astrologer Atrush did indeed come true: Rabiah was as shining as the light of a star to the world, and she met with a tragic death.[56]

The people of Afghanistan continues to honor the memory of Rabiah Balkhi. A newly established high school for young girls bears her name. The Republic of Afghanistan has recently decided to produce a movie based on the life and work of Rabiah Balkhi as part of a renewal of national interest in preserving the historical and cultural heritage of the Afghan people.

(Germantown, Fall 1988)

---

[55] Zhobal, Mohammed H. *Tarikh-i Adabyat-i Dari dar Afghanistan*. Kabul: Ministry of Education Printing House, 1956, pp. 82-83.

[56] Fernea, Elizabeth Warnock and Beziegan, Basima Qattan. *Middle Eastern Muslim Women Speak*. University of Texas Press, 1984, p. 80.

The Excerpts of Rabiah Balkhi's Poems

RABIAH BALKHI wrote her poetry in both Arabic and Persian (Dari), and sometimes she used both languages in a single writing.[57] Her style of writing is known as the ghazal.[58] This is a type of stanza in which each line contains a complete thought. The thoughts are not necessarily related and do not depend on each other for explanation or clarity. Of the many poems, which Rabiah Balkhi supposedly wrote, only a limited number of excerpts have been preserved.

The following excerpt was written as a protest toward the uncaring attitude shown by her lover:

My prayer to God is this:
that you be bound in love with someone
Unmoving as stick and stone.

For only having suffered love's agony
of pain and separation
Shall you come to feel and value
my love for you.[59]

This excerpt is one in which she expresses her wonderment at the beauty and perfection of spring:

The fresh roses are such a lovely
company, in beauty and splendor,
They surpass the celebrated
paintings of the inimitable Mani.

---

[57] Rypka, Jan. *History of Iranian Literature*. Dordrecht: D. Reidel, 1968, p. 144.
[58] Farviar, Hussain. *Tarikh-i Adabyat-i Iran wa Tarikh-i Shu'ara*. Teheran, 1962, p. 96.
[59] Safa, Zabih Allah. *Tarikh-i Adabyat dar Iran*. Teheran, 1967, p. 451.

The roses have put on the fairest
colors from Leila's face;
For not otherwise would the eyes
of Majnoon behold them from the clouds.
Night has so filled the tulips with
her wine, that in the dawn
Flush they sway like ruby chalices.

The narcissus blooms carry the
tint of silver and gold,
Each of them looking like a crown
fit to adorn a princely head.

The frail violets appareled in
their dedicate hues,
Look like a company of nuns
receiving their ordination from nature.[60]

The last excerpt is probably one of her best known, for it is the poem
that she supposedly wrote upon the wall of the public bath with her
own life's blood. She addressed to her brother, Haris:

You judged my love a sin,
you have been my undoing;
With what heart shall you face up to God,
in the hour of questioning?

The glories of this world and more,
without him are as little;
But Hell, if he were with me,
I should willingly embrace.

The wiseman's saying comes true.
Sooner or later, pride has its fall.[61]

---

[60] Safa, Zabih Allah. *Tarikh-i Adabyat dar Iran*. Teheran, 1967, p. 451.
[61] IBID, p. 451.

Helen Keller
(1880 – 1968)

(Source: makar.us)

Helen Keller was a women's-rights activist, a socialist, and a world-famous celebrity. She was dedicated to helping the blind and handicapped, raising funds for the blind, and lobbying for commissions for the blind. Helen Keller received many honorary degrees.

Born: June 27, 1880 in Tuscumbia, Alabama
Died: June 1, 1968 (aged 87) in Arcan Ridge, Westport, Connecticut
Parents: Captain Arthur H. Keller and Kate Adams Keller
Education: Bachelor of Arts (1904), Radcliffe College, Cambridge, Massachusetts; an honorary degree by Harvard University (1955)
Her teachers: Dr. Samuel Gridley Howe, Anne Mansfield Sullivan, and Miss Fuller.
Companions/Secretary: Anne Mansfield Sullivan (died in October 20, 1936) and Polly Thomson (died in 1960)
Political activities: A member of Socialist Party
Social activities: An activist of Industrial Workers of the World (IWW); a fundraiser for the American Foundation for the Blind
Foundations: Helen Keller International (1915); American Civil Liberties Union [ACLU] (1920)

Awards: The Presidential Medal of Freedom (1964) by President
    Lyndon B. Johnson; the Women's Hall of Fame (1965)
Books: The Story of My Life (1903), The World I Live In (1908),
    Out of the Dark (1913), My Religion (1927) [re-issued as Light
    in my Darkness], Midstream: My Later Life (1929), Helen
    Keller's Journal (1938), Let Us Have Faith (1940), Teacher
    (1955)

(Source: MSN Encarta)

HELEN KELLER was an American author, activist, and lecturer.
She was the first deaf-blind female to graduate from college. In her
lifetime, she campaigned for women's suffrage, workers' rights,
socialism and progressive causes. As a prolific author, she was well
traveled and was outspoken in her opposition to war.

Helen Keller was born in Tuscumbia, Alabama in June 27, 1880.
She was a pretty baby; happy and smart. When Helen was six
months old, she began talking. But a year later, in February 1882,
she suffered a terrible sickness. She had a high fever. Her parents
and doctors were afraid she would die. After a few days the illness
was gone, but Helen turned away from bright lights. The illness had
left Helen totally blind and deaf.

Because Helen could not hear other people speak, she did not learn to talk herself. She forgot the few words she knew as a baby. Helen did things with her hands to tell people what she wanted. Helen touched things to know how they felt and how they were shaped.

When Helen was five, her mother read about a woman named Laura Bridgman, who was also deaf and blind. She had been taught to read and write, and to "talk" to people by using a finger alphabet. Her teacher was Dr. Samuel Gridley Howe, of the Perkins Institute for the Blind, in Boston, Massachusetts.[62] Laura Bridgman's story gave the Kellers hope that something could be done for Helen. Her parents took her to eye doctors in Baltimore, Maryland, but nothing could be done to help Helen see again. Then Helen's parents took her to Washington, D.C. to meet Dr. Alexander Graham Bell,[63] the inventor of the telephone. Dr. Bell had once taught in a school for the deaf. He helped the Kellers find a teacher for Helen. He advised Mr. Keller to get in touch with Michael Anagnos, the director of the Perkins Institution for the Blind in Boston, Massachusetts. Mr. Anagnos replied to his letter and said he would try to find a suitable teacher for Helen. The teacher they found was Anne Mansfield Sullivan, a former student at Perkins. Helen first met Anne Mansfield Sullivan on March 3, 1887 at her parents' house.

(Source: Wikipedia - Helen Keller in 1905)

---

[62] Sabin, Francene: *The Courage of Helen Keller*. New Jersey: Troll Associates, 1982, p.17.
[63] Dr. Alexander Graham Bell (1847-1922) was an eminent scientist, inventor, and innovator who was credited with the invention of the telephone.

First, Anne Sullivan taught Helen proper manners. Then she taught her words. Anne used a finger alphabet. Anne took Helen's hands and put it under the water. In Helen's other hand Anne spelled "w-a-t-e-r." Many years later Helen wrote that learning "w-a-t-e-r," her first word, gave her soul light, hope, and joy.[64] Helen learned hundreds, then thousands of words. Soon Anne Sullivan taught Helen to read by feeling patterns of raised dots on paper. This kind of writing for the blind is called Braille.[65] Helen learned so much and so fast that she became famous throughout the world. Helen was completely deaf but she could feel vibrations. When she learned that a blind-deaf girl in Norway had learned to speak Helen decided that she had to learn as well. Helen did learn to speak when she was ten years old. A teacher called Miss Fuller was found and began to show Helen how sounds were made by putting Helen's fingers inside her mouth to feel how the tongue and lips moved to produce each sound. Helen learned well but she couldn't hear the sounds she was making.

Helen became a friendly and generous child. When she learned that a little blind-deaf boy called Tommy Stringer was too poor to go to a special school she was very upset. She set up a special fund and sent Tommy to Perkins. Helen has begun to show how much she could care for others. Annie continued to take her on interesting trips and to meet famous people. Helen met the writer Mark Twain,[66] who became a great admirer of hers.

(Source: Wikipedia - Helen Keller with Anne Sullivan in 1888)

---

[64] Adler, David A.: *A Picture Book of Helen Keller*. New York: Holiday House, 1990, p.17.

[65] Tames, Richard: *Helen Keller*. New York: Franklin Watts Inc., 1989, p.12.

[66] Mark Twain, a pen name of Samuel Langhorne Clements (1835-1910,) was a famous American writer, novelist, humorist, satirist and lecturer in the nineteenth century.

Helen thoroughly enjoyed learning and decided to go to college. In 1990 Helen became a college student. She went to Radcliffe College, the women's section of Harvard University, in Cambridge, Massachusetts. Anne Sullivan sat next to her and spelled in Helen's hand everything that was said in class. She took classes in French, German, English, Greek, Latin, Roman History, algebra, geometry, physics, economics, philosophy and astronomy.[67] Helen was an excellent student. While she was in college, she wrote *The Story of My Life* and it was published in 1903,[68] which was read by people throughout the world. In 1904 Helen graduated and won her the degree of Bachelor of Arts with honors.[69]

Helen wrote more articles and books about her life, her teacher (Anne Sullivan), and how she learned. In 1905 she took up her first public appointment as a member of the Massachusetts Commission for the Blind. In 1913 Helen published a book of essays on socialism, which called *Out of the Dark*. She and Anne Sullivan lectured before large audiences. By 1914, Helen and Anne hired Polly Thomson, a young girl from Scotland, to help them make all the complicated arrangements for travel and hotels and lecture halls. Helen had worked so hard on her speech that she could talk at public meetings. The same year Helen spoke out strongly against the United States getting involved the World War I.

(Source: Wikipedia - Keller and Sullivan in 1898)

---

[67] Keller, Helen: *The Story of My Life by Helen Keller.* New York: Bantam Book, 1990, p.69.

[68] Kudlinski, Kathleen V.: *Helen Keller: A Light for the Blind.* New York: Puffin Books, 1989, p.31.

[69] Tames, Richard: *Helen Keller.* New York: Franklin Watts Inc., 1989, p.16.

Helen's lecture tour was such a success that she had to employ another secretary to help her with all the letters she received. His name was Peter Fagan. After a short time working together, he told her that he wanted to marry her. When Peter came to the Kellers' house in Tuscumbia he was sent away at gunpoint. He never came back.

In 1918 a studio in Hollywood offered to make a movie about Helen's life. The movie was called *Deliverance*. Unfortunately, it was not a great success and so Helen and Annie still needed to make money. They decided to tell their story themselves on the stage. Helen and Annie worked out an act and toured the vaudeville theaters, which presented comedians, dancers, animal acts and conjurors.

In 1927 Helen published a book called *My Religion*, which explained how she had been influenced by the ideas of Emanuel Swedenborg[70] who argued that logic and science proved the existence of God. In 1929 Helen published *Midstream: My Later Life*, which brought her biography up to date.

In 1932 Helen took the lead in organizing a World Conference for the Blind. In 1933 Annie's life story, written by Nella, was published. In October 1936 Annie had an operation on her remaining eye. It was unsuccessful and the strain of the operation led to her death on October 20, 1936. She had been with Helen for almost fifty years.

After Anne's death, Polly Thomson,[71] Helen's secretary since 1914, became her constant companion. Helen worked all her life to help others, especially blind people. She worked for many years for the American Foundation for the Blind.[72]

---

[70] Emanuel Swedenborg, born Emanuel Swedberg (1688-1772), was a Swedish scientist, philosopher, Christian mystic, and theologian.
[71] Polly Thomson died in 1960.
[72] Adler, David A.: *A Picture Book of Helen Keller*. New York: Holiday House, 1990, p.25.

During the World War II, Helen visited injured soldiers in hospitals. Her visits meant a lot to the soldiers. Many of them had been blinded or had lost their hearing in the fighting. Helen brought them hope. She also met kings, queens, presidents, actors, writers, and scientists.[73]

In 1953 a new movie about Helen's life was released. It was called *The Unconquered* and won an Academy Award. In 1955 Helen published her own account of Annie's life and work. It was called simply *Teacher*. The same year she was awarded an honorary degree by Harvard University. In 1957 a play about Helen, *The Miracle Worker*, performed its first production. It was a great success and became a prize-winning movie.

Helen's eightieth birthday was an occasion for many tributes. Leading newspapers reviewed her life's achievements. At her birthday luncheon, Helen presented the first Helen Keller International Award to the blind Colonel Baker, head of the Canadian Institute for the Blind. Then she went back to her old college, Radcliffe, to dedicate the Anne Sullivan Memorial Fountain.

Many people, universities, and governments all over the world gave Helen awards. In 1964 President Lyndon B. Johnson gave her the Presidential Medal of Freedom. Helen Keller died on June 1, 1968 at the age of eighty-eight.

***

Helen Keller couldn't see or hear, but for more than eighty years she had always been busy. She read and wrote books. She learned how to swim and ride a bicycle. But most of all, her bravery, brilliance, and spirit brought hope and love to millions of handicapped people.

(Germantown, Spring 1996)

---

[73]   IBID, p.28.

Golda Meir
(1898 – 1978)

(Source: Wikipedia)

Born: Goldie Mabovitch, May 3, 1898 in Kiev, Russia
Died: December 8, 1978 (aged 80) in Jerusalem, Israel
Hebrew name: Meir ('to burn brightly') in 1956
Parents: Moshe Mabovitch (carpenter) and Blume Naidtich
Immigration: Golda emigrated with her family to Milwaukee,
Wisconsin in 1906
Marriage: 1917 – 1951. Husband: Morris Meyerson (died in 1951)
Political party: Mapai (Israel Workers Party), Alignment
Political activities:
   * Prime Minister of Israel: March 17, 1969 – June 3, 1974
   * Secretary General of Mapai: 1966
   * Foreign Affairs Minister of Israel: 1956 – 1966
   * Minister of Labour of Israel: 1949 - 1956
   * Ambassador to Moscow: 1948
   * Executive Committee of the Histadrut: 1934
   * Emissary in the United States: 1932 - 1934
   * Secretary of Moetzet HaPoalot (Working Women's Council):
     1928
   * Labor Zionist Organization (The Poalei Zion): 1915

(Source: Wikipedia - Golda Meir at Merhavia)

GOLDA MEIR is one of the greatest women of the 20th century. This amazing woman was born in Russia and brought up in Milwaukee (U.S.), and later became the Prime Minister of Israel. Golda Meir is one of the political giants of our time. She was also a shopkeeper, school teacher, librarian, farmer, fundraiser, hunger striker, and freedom fighter. She lived a life filled with extraordinary events, towering achievement, hope, courage, and conviction.

***

Golda Meir was born on May 3, 1898 in Kiev, Russia. Golda immigrated to America with her family when she was eight (1906). She was raised in Milwaukee' Jewish community. Golda was headstrong even as a young girl, constantly fighting with her parents and challenging her teachers. At the age of fifteen she ran away to be with her sister (Sheyna) in Denver, Colorado, to start life on her own.

As a young woman, Golda Meir had great beauty, a full, firm figure, long lustrous hair, and a magnetic sparkle when she threw her head back to laugh. The love affairs she had were with men of power, the pioneering giants for her time. They had opened doors for her, pushed her career, but she still had to prove herself, again and again. And she did. In this tight society, managed by men, she was the only woman, the only American, to break into inner circle. Yet though she was so strong-willed, her letters to these men she loved were passionate and tender, and make clear her longing and her loneliness.

The greatest of all was her love affair with Israel. She yearned to see Palestine returned to the Jews, and she was willing to fight for it for the rest of her life. She settled in Tel Aviv, and then moved to a kibbutz.[74] In Golda's vision, the kibbutz would form the spiritual core of the homeland. The idea was that the kibbutz would help their people grow into a nation living on their own soil as of right and not on sufferance, living in houses they had built, and eating food they had grown.

Later she traveled the world to raise desperately needed money and worked closely with David Ben-Gurion [75] to mobilize the Israeli army. David Ben-Gurion, the leader of the Jews in Palestine and the first Prime Minister of Israel, said of Golda, "Someday, when history will be written, it will be said that there was a Jewish woman who got the money which made the State possible." She lived through the fighting and the shelling of Jerusalem. She lived to join those who signed Israel's Declaration of Independence.[76] Israel was declared a state on May 14, 1948.

---

[74] Golda Meir: *My Life By Golda Meir*. New York: G. P. Putnam's Sons, 1975, pp. 86-93.

[75] David A. Adler: *Our Golda - The Story of Golda Meir*. New York: The Viking Press, 1984, p. 43.

[76] IBID, p. 45

Golda Meir was Israel's first Ambassador to Russia. When David Ben-Gurion became Prime Minister, the leader of the new nation, he asked Golda to be Israel's first Minister of Labor. In 1956 Ben-Gurion asked Golda to become Foreign Minister. In February 1969 Golda was selected as Israel's new Prime Minister. After five years as Prime Minister, Golda Meir resigned in 1974.

At the end of her life, asked to name the most formative forces that shaped her, she answered: *"Childhood in Russia, which means poverty, pogroms, and political repression. Parents and elder sister - trade unionism from my parents, socialism from my sister. My husband, which means everything I have learned to enjoy in the world of culture: poetry, music, books, ideas."* [77] She died in 1978 at the age of eighty.

(Source: Wikipedia - Memorial plaque in Kiev)

Golda Meir once admitted of her private life, *"I was no nun."* She was also no saint. Her critics were many and there were black holes in her life. But this was a woman who lived in a state of emergency, paid her dues, earned her greatness. Out of her strength, she helped create a nation; out of her spirit, she helped mold a population. If Israel had a voice in the world, it was the voice of Golda Meir.

(Germantown, Spring 1996)

---

[77] Martin, Ralph G. *Golda Meir: The Romantic Years*. New York: Charles Scribner's Sons, 1988, p. 82.

Sam Houston
(1793 - 1863)

(Source: Wikipedia)

Sam Houston was one of the Founding Fathers of Texas. He was a commander-in-chief of the Texas army, the first president of the Texas Republic, and later governor of Texas.

Born: March 2, 1793 in Rockbridge County, Virginia
Died: July 26, 1863 (aged 70) in Huntsville, Texas
Indian name: The Raven
Nicknames: The Big Drunk, The Old Dragon, The Great Designer, The Hero of San Jacinto, Six Feet Six
Parents: Major Samuel Houston and Elizabeth Paxton
Spouse: Eliza Allen (1828 – 1837), Tiana Rogers Gentry (1829 – 1832), and Margaret Moffette Lea (1840 – 1863)
Children: 8 (with Margaret)
Religion: Baptist
Military (1812 – 1818): Lieutenant
Political activities:
    Governor of Texas (1859 – 1861)

U.S. Senator (1845 – 1859)

President of the Republic of Texas (1836 – 1838; 1841 – 1844)

Commander-in-chief (1836)

Major General, the Texas Army (1835)

Representative for Nacogdoches at the Convention of 1833

Governor of Tennessee (1827 – 1829)

Congressman, Tennessee, The House of Representatives (1822 – 1827)

Attorney General, Nashville district, Tennessee (1818)

A command in the state militia (1818)

An Indian agent to the Cherokees (1817)

SAM HOUSTON was one of the Founding Fathers of Texas. He was commander-in-chief of the Texas army, first president of the Republic of Texas, and later governor of the state. During his lifetime Sam Houston acquired friends, enemies, and a variety of nicknames: the Big Drunk, the Old Dragon, the Great Designer, the Hero of San Jacinto, Six Feet Six, etc. Sam Houston was a 19th century American statesman, politician, and soldier.

What was Sam Houston doing in the years before he went to Texas? What was his sense of humor and humanness? What was his personality? Why must we know about him? Let me find the answers.

Childhood

Sam Houston was born on March 2, 1793 at Timber Ridge plantation, Virginia. Sam had four brothers and three sisters. They had a fine time growing up on the big plantation together. They rode horseback, swam in Mill Creek, and fought imaginary Indians and Red Coats. Their father built a school for them and some of the neighbor's children. Sam was the poorest student. He played hooky regularly. He liked to read about battles and to look at maps. When his father was promoted to major he was delighted.

When San Houston was thirteen years old his father announced that he was going to sell their plantation home in Virginia and take the family to Tennessee. Sam Houston thought himself the luckiest boy in the world. Tennessee! Here was a great adventure. Fights with Indians, perhaps! He thought that someday the Indians would be his friends. He would live with them and speak their language. A Cherokee chieftain would adopt him as his son and call him The Raven.

New Adventure

One afternoon a fine new wagon and a team of five horses drove up to the plantation. Major Houston announced proudly that he had bought the wagon to transport his family to their new home in Tennessee.

In the midst of the packing Major Houston left home to resign from the Army. On his way back he was taken ill at a roadside tavern and died. Sam Houston never saw him again. The plantation had been sold and the wagons packed, but without their brave father.

Three weeks after the Houston's farewells had been said in Virginia the new five-horse wagon and the old four-horse wagon, dusty and battered from the trip across the Alleghenies, reached the collection of log houses known as Knoxville, the capital of Tennessee. Ten miles farther lay the land bought by Major Houston before he died. It was called the Baker's Creek Valley on the Big Smoky Mountains.

The house stood near a cool mountain spring on a shelf of land sloping away in three directions. This was Sam's favorite spot. He could sit by the spring and gaze for miles around the countryside. Sometimes Sam would take his rifle and a book and be gone for days at a time, living on squirrel or wild turkey that he killed and cooked over an open fire. He met Indians on his wanderings. He found them very friendly and amiable. The Indians told him that the white people had come and taken their lands and started the trouble.

Sam's brothers disapproved most heartily of Sam's making friends with the Indians. His mother did not believe that Sam was a wayward boy. He was such a likable young scamp, the handsomest of the Houston boys. He was fair and tall. He had wavy chestnut hair and friendly blue eyes.

Sam tried his best to please his mother, but he just could not stick to farming. One evening Sam strolled away from Maryville with a book under his arm and a rifle on his shoulder. His brothers started out to find him two days later. Sam was living with the Indian chief as his invited guest. He liked these Indians. They were not always quarreling with him or among themselves like the white people. Finally, Sam did go back to his family for a short period.

In The Army

Sam Houston joined the Regular Army at the age of nineteen. Within thirty days he was a drill sergeant. In four months he was commissioned as an ensign and transferred to the 39th Infantry.

After a year of careful preparation, the 39th Regiment took the field. They were sent against a strong tribe of Creek Indians in Alabama. Ensign Sam Houston was wounded in battle. He was sent home for treatment for a while.

It was nearly a year before Ensign Houston was well enough to rejoin his regiment. He was immediately promoted to second lieutenant and transferred to New Orleans. He was taken ill again and went by sea to a military hospital in New York for treatment. He then transferred to Nashville, Tennessee, for light duty at the headquarters of General Jackson.

The General sent him to persuade the Indians and requested that they should leave Tennessee and avert the war. Sam Houston discussed the treaty with the Indians.

Finally, Sam disagreed with John C. Calhoun, the Secretary of War, and resigned from the Army on March 1, 1818. The reason of his resignation is that *"he could not honorably stay under the command of a secretary of war who had shown him such disrespect."* ("dressed like a savage" before the secretary of war). [78] He returned to Tennessee and became a close friend of Andrew Jackson. [79]

A Grown Person

In Nashville, Sam Houston had begun to study laws. In six months Sam passed an examination for admission to the bar. He moved to Lebanon, 30 miles from Nashville, to open a law office. After a while Governor McMinn made the appointment of Sam Houston as adjutant-general of the militia.

One morning Sam received a visitor's call. It was Sam's Cherokee friend John Rogers. The visit almost changed Houston's career. John Rogers told him about the treaty, but the government once more had failed them. The Cherokee needed Sam's help.

General Andrew Jackson offered to endorse his nomination for prosecuting attorney for the district of Nashville. Sam did not go to the Indian country, but to the prosecuting attorney's office. Later Sam Houston was promoted a major general of the Tennessee militia. Then Gen. Jackson sent him to Washington, D.C. as a congressman.

After William Carroll retired from the governorship of Tennessee, Sam Houston was promoted as a candidate. He was elected governor. Sam Houston was made a new kind of governor. He was a governor that nearly every man, woman, and child had talked to.

---

[78] Fritz, Jean: Make Way for Sam Houston. New York: G.P. Putnam's Sons, 1986, p. 19.

[79] Andrew Jackson later became the 7th President of the United States (1829-1837).

One day Sam fell in love. The girl was Eliza Allen. She was seventeen years old. They were married at Eliza's home on January 22, 1829. One day Sam found out that his wife did not love him because she still loved her boyhood friend. Finally, Sam and his wife had separated. She went back to her father's house. Sam Houston abandoned his campaign for reelection. He also resigned his office and went to the West. He stayed with the Indians who loved him and believed in him.

His Future Home

After a life of adventure that would have been enough for ten ordinary people, Sam Houston plunged into the greatest adventure of his career. One day Sam Houston said farewell to his Indian friends and turned to Texas. He made his future home in that great country. His life there was a most thrilling one – wars with the Mexicans and battles in politics.

With a tattered little army, outnumbered nearly two to one, Sam Houston won the battle at San Jacinto. Texas emerged as the great Lone Star Republic. Through Sam Houston's resolute efforts, Texas became a state in the Union. Sam Houston was elected the first President of the Texas Republic and later the governor of Texas. The capital city was named in his honor. Sam Houston died on July 26, 1863 in Huntsville, Tennessee. He was seventy years old.

***

Sam Houston's life is a splendid story for boys and girls. It is a story of adventure, a story of courage and wisdom, a story of honor and patriotism, etc. These stories will hold their attention. Each story is a great saga. It throws light upon a period apt to be skimmed hastily in the study of American history. I did learn courage and honor from Sam Houston.

(Germantown, Spring 1987)

PART III: SOCIETY, POLITICS, AND RELIGION

The Concept of "America" and Being "American" in the 1750's and 1760's

(Source: Wikipedia - Franklin in 1783, an engraving from a painting by Joseph Duplessis)

According to Walter Isaacson, in *"Observations Concerning the Increase of Mankind"* (1751), Benjamin Franklin *"observed that the colonist were only half as likely as the English to remain unmarried, that they married younger (around age 20), and that they averaged twice as many children (approximately eight). Thus, he concluded, America's population would double every twenty years and surpass that of England in one hundred years."* [80] Benjamin Franklin was right. By 1851, the American population surpassed that of England. Beside his political tracts, Benjamin Franklin believed that the increased productivity of American would be able to supply the population growth.

---

[80] Isaacson, Walter: Benjamin Franklin: An American Life. New York: Simon & Schuster, 2003, p. 150.

From 1751 through to 1763, as Postmaster General, Benjamin Franklin [81] traveled over nearly every post road in America. He visited southern planters, stopped overnight with farmers, and talked with pioneers. As a result of his travels, Benjamin Franklin knew how Americans lived and what they were thinking. According to Benjamin Franklin, by the 1750's and 1760's people in the New World were beginning to think of themselves as "*Americans*."

By the 1760's there were more than 2 millions people in all the British colonies who lived along the Atlantic seaboard. Throughout the colonies, the majority of the people lived in the country, but in the South the proportion of country dwellers was especially high. Most of the southern people lived on small farms. Some lived on the frontier in small clearings cut from the forest. The wealthy planters lived on the fertile coastal plains. Most of the planters' luxuries came from England. They seemed more like Englishmen than Americans.

Like the southern planters, the wealthier townspeople in all the colonies dressed and acted like wealthier Englishmen in the Old Country. Most of the colonial cities and towns were seaports, and their ties with England were close indeed. The influence of the Old World could be seen in many other features of town life. In some ways the colonial towns were different from the towns of England. For one thing, people from many different nations were learning to live together in colonial America. The colonial towns, as well as the frontier and farming areas, were "melting pots." The "melting pot" of colonial America was also producing a new American vocabulary. The townspeople mixed English with American ideas.

---

[81]   Benjamin Franklin was the Founding Father, scientist, inventor, diplomat, writer, and business strategist. He was the only person to sign all four of its founding papers: the Declaration of Independence (July 4, 1776), the Treaty of Paris (September 3, 1783), the Peace of Paris (November 30, 1783), and the Constitution (September 17, 1787).

The greatest difference between English and American towns can be summed up in the word "*opportunity*." There was plenty of work for everyone in any of the colonial towns.

The area of America that was most different from the Old World lay back from the seacoast. Not far from the coast, there were many small farming villages. These pioneer farmers were self-sufficient from necessity. In the minds of these self-reliant pioneer farmers, certain ideas began to take root and grow. The pioneers were free persons. They were individualists. Their success depended on their own strength and skill. They believed in the value of *cooperation*. They felt themselves to be the equals of other people. Finally, they were optimists. They were beginning to think of themselves as "*Americans*."

The most "*American*" of all the colonists were the pioneers. Every year, in all colonies, hundreds of adventurous youths left their homes to find excitement in the western forests. They shed many traces of European civilization. They explored the "*no man's land*" between civilization and savagery. They were individualists. They were brimming with the spirit of independence, self-reliance, and initiative. Their individualism, however, was cooperative as well as competitive. Frontier life was a wonderful process of mixing many people with different backgrounds into a new, independent kind of person. Their idea of *equality* – which was the core of democracy – took root and grew swiftly.

The pioneer farmers and the frontier persons changed much more rapidly. Because they had so few ties with England, they became much more American than they were English. The pioneer farmers and the frontier persons were becoming more and more democratic in their ways of living and thinking. The democratic ideas took root in colonial America. We call them "*the American way of life*."

(Germantown, Fall 2004)

Nathaniel Hawthorne
(1804 – 1864)

(Source: Wikipedia)

NATHANIEL HAWTHORNE was the first American romance writer.

Born: July 4, 1804 in Salem, Massachusetts
Died: May 19, 1864 on a brief vacation with Franklin Pierce in Plymouth, New Hampshire.
Father: Nathaniel Hathorne, Sr.
Spouse: Sophia Peabody of Salem (1842 – 1864)
Children: 3 (Una, Julian, and Rose)
Education: Bachelor degree, Bowdoin College in Maine
Political Party: Democrat
Books: *Fanshawe: A Tale* (a novel, 1828)
    The Hollow of the Three Hills (a story, 1830)
    My Kinsman, Major Molineux (the tales, 1832)
    Young Goodman Brown (the tales, 1835)
    The Gray Champion (short stories, 1835)
    The White Old Maid (short stories, 1835)
    The Minister's Black Veil (the tales, 1836)
    The Maypole of Merry Mount (the tales, 1836)
    Twice-Told Tales (short stories, 1837)
    The Great Carbuncle (short stories, 1837)

Dr. Heidegger's Experiment (short stories, 1837)
The Birth-Mark (the tales, 1843)
Rappaccini's Daughter (the tales, 1844)
The Artist of the Beautiful (short stories, 1844)
P.'s Correspondence (short stories, 1845)
Mosses from an Old Manse (short stories, 1846)
The Scarlet Letter (a novel, 1850)
Ethan Brand (short stories, 1850)
The House of Seven Gables (a novel, 1851)
The Blithedale Romance (a novel, 1852)
The Snow-Image, and Other Twice-Told Tales (short stories, 1852)
A Wonder-Book for Girls and Boys (short stories, 1852)
Tanglewood Tales (the tales, 1853)
Feathertop (short stories, 1854)
The Marble Faun (a novel, 1860)
The Dolliver Romance (a novel, 1863)

Two Basic Differences between Transcendentalism and Anti-transcendentalism

The points of view of Transcendentalism and Anti-transcendentalism are totally different and opposite. Two basic differences between Transcendentalism and Anti-transcendentalism are *not* *evil* or *optimism* and *evil* or *pessimism*. I will discuss these differences in the writings of one transcendental writer (Ralph Waldo Emerson, an *optimist*) and one anti-transcendental writer (Nathaniel Hawthorne, a *pessimist*).

***

Transcendental writer

One of the most famous transcendental writers is Ralph Waldo Emerson.[82] He praised nature and man. According to his philosophy and writing, *"man is connected to nature."* He believed very much in imagination.

In his book, *Nature*, [83] Emerson defined *nature* as follows: *"Nature, in its ministry to man, is not only the material, but is also the process and result."* [84] Emerson affirmed, *"In the wilderness, I find something more dear and connate [related] than in streets or villages. In the tranquil landscape, and especially in the distant line of the horizon, man beholds somewhat as beautiful as his own nature."* [85] His belief in the whole, *"Nothing is quite beautiful alone: nothing but is beautiful in the whole."* [86] He compared the art and the nature as follows: *"The poet, the painter, the sculptor, the musician, the architect seek each to concentrate this radiance of the world on one point, and each in his several work to satisfy the love of beauty which stimulates him to produce. This is Art, a nature passed through the alembic of man. Thus in art, does nature work through the will of a man filled with the beauty of her works."* [87]

(Source: pbs.org)

---

[82] Ralph Waldo Emerson (1803-1882) was a famous American poet in the 19th century. He was an essayist, a philosopher, an orator and a lecturer. He was also known as a transcendental poet. He was a founder of Transcendentalism. He supported the abolitionism.

[83] *Nature* was published in 1836.

[84] The Norton Anthology of American Literature, Fifth Edition/Volume I. W.W. Norton & Company, New York (1998), p. 1076.

[85] IBID, p. 1075.

[86] IBID, p. 1080.

[87] IBID, p. 1080.

According to Emerson, Man is not evil. Man is good. He believed "man is in God" and "God is in man." Man is a part of God and God is a part of man. Man is not evil but good. In his book, *Nature*, Emerson affirmed that: *"I am [a] part or particle of God."* [88] The gap between God and man is very small. Emerson saw no evil in man: *"evil is no more seen."* [89] According to his philosophy, the individual is very important. Man is self-reliant. On the other hand, he is a pantheist. He proposed a new kind of knowledge and favored social reform. He was an *optimist*.

Anti-transcendental writer

One of the most famous anti-transcendental writers is Nathaniel Hawthorne.[90] The world, in his point of view, is unshaped. His society was full of unrest. Hawthorne believed that man is evil. Evil is inside a man. Evil is hard to escape. In *The Scarlet Letter* [91], there is evil and a Satan in Chillingworth. In Hester's prison cell, Chillingworth convinces her to promise that she will not reveal that he is her lawful husband. He asks her to keep this vow because he does not wish to suffer *"the dishonor that besmirches the husband of a faithless woman."* [92]

According to Hawthorne, *"the philosopher seeking an honest man, but with no better fortune."* [93] Only God is good. Man needs God's grace. A gap between Man and God is very large. Hawthorne is a *pessimist*.

***

---

[88] IBID, p. 1075.
[89] IBID, p. 1101.
[90] Nathaniel Hawthorne (1804-1864) was the first American romance writer. He was a descendant of Puritan ancestors.
[91] *The Scarlet Letter*, a novel, was published in 1850.
[92] IBID, p. 1347.
[93] IBID, p. 1227.

Transcendentalism, especially that followed by writers such as Ralph Waldo Emerson, favored nature and optimism. Man is connected to nature. Man is good. God is in man and man is in God. On the other hand, Anti-transcendentalism, especially Nathaniel Hawthorne, favored God and spirit. Man is evil. Nature is violent and unrest.

(Germantown, Fall 1998)

(Source: Wikipedia)

Ralph Waldo Emerson (1803 – 1882) was a famous American poet in the 19th century. He was an essayist, a philosopher, an orator and a lecturer. He was also known as a transcendental poet. He was a founder of Transcendentalism. He supported the abolitionism.

The Monroe Doctrine

(Source: ourdocuments.gov)

The war of 1812 (between America and Great Britain) [94] had no winner. Neither side could be called victorious, but it did give the Americans confidence in themselves. The Treaty of Ghent (1814) [95] merely declared that the two countries were now at peace with each other. Boundaries were to remain just as before the war. The one result of this new self-confidence was the famous Monroe Doctrine.[96] It was issued a few years after the war. The Doctrine explained the United States' policy toward European interference in the America.

***

The Holly Alliance Threatened the New Republics

After the war of 1812, the American government soon learned that the life of the new nation was threatened by a group of strong European rulers. It was called the Holy Alliance. The French Revolutions had frightened these European kings and emperors. They had agreed to help one another put down all attempts by the people of Europe to set up free governments. They even promised to help the Spanish king get back his lost American colonies.

Great Britain was the only powerful European country that had refused to join the Holy Alliance. The British people did have something to say about their government. They did not want to help despotic rulers keep down the people in other countries. Like the United States, Britain had already recognized the Old Spanish colonies as independent and enjoyed trading with them.

---

[94] The war of 1812 was fought between the United States of America and the United Kingdom of Great Britain and Ireland. The war was fought from 1812 to 1815, although a peace treaty was signed in 1814.

[95] The Treaty of Ghent was signed on December 24, 1814 in Ghent, Belgium. It was the peace treaty that ended the war of 1812 between the United States of America and the United Kingdom of Great Britain and Ireland.

[96] The Monroe Doctrine has functioned as a declaration of hegemony and a right of unilateral intervention over the Western Hemisphere.

The British government suggested that the United States and Britain should act together to keep the Holy Alliance from interfering in South America. President James Monroe [97] called on his cabinet for advice. President Monroe and John Quincy Adams [98], Secretary of State, decided that it was better for the United States to act alone, without joining Britain. President Monroe hoped the United States, as the oldest and strongest country, would be the leader. So, on December 2, 1823, President James Monroe addressed to the 18th Congress (his seventh annual State of the Union Address to Congress) and he warned the European powers (Spain and France) not to interfere in the affairs of the Western Hemisphere (the newly independent nations of the Americas). That message was known as the Monroe Doctrine.

The Monroe Doctrine

In this famous message, President James Monroe made four clear declarations:

1. The Western Hemisphere was no longer open to colonization by European powers.

2. Any attempt by any European countries to establish colonies in the New World or to gain political control of any American countries would be viewed as the manifestation of an unfriendly disposition toward the United States.

3. The United States would not meddle in European affairs or in the affairs of American colonies already established.

4. In return, Europe must not in any way disturb the political status of any free American countries.

Enforcing the Doctrine

---

[97] James Monroe, the fifth president of the United States (1817-1825)
[98] John Quincy Adams, the sixth president of the United States (1825-1829)

With the Monroe Doctrine the United States proclaimed a policy of an "America for Americans." The Latin Americans supported the Americans to the south, as well as by Great Britain. The Latin Americans recognized that the Monroe Doctrine guaranteed their independence from Europe.

Great Britain, especially the British navy, gave the Monroe Doctrine its real strength. In 1823, the British fleet controlled the Atlantic sea-lanes. It was only with British consent that the ships of any nation, including the United States, moved between Europe and the Americas. It was America's good fortune that British merchants were keenly interested in preserving the independence of the countries of Central and South America. At the first hint of interference from the Holy Alliance, Great Britain sided with the Americas.

Significance of the Doctrine

The Monroe Doctrine was a direct warning to Russia, France, Spain, and to other European powers that the United States was vitally concerned in the affairs of all the nations in North, Central, and South America. It became a cornerstone of United States foreign policy.

The Monroe Doctrine also revealed the growing spirit of American strength and unity. In 1823 it meant that President Monroe spoke for the united people. He spoke for a nation that was determined to retain its hard-won independence from Europe and to decide its own policies in its own way.

***

In later years, the Monroe Doctrine was to be applied many times. The Monroe Doctrine is still an important part of the United Sates' foreign policy.

(Germantown, Spring 1997)

Pirates in The Gulf of Thailand

(Source: boatpeople75.tripod.com)

We're living in a high-tech society, where people are civilized. But pirates still exist in some places around the world. Raping, killing, abducting, robbing, attacking, shooting, knifing, beating, and ramming are the main activities of pirates.

Since the fall of Saigon in 1975, there were over three million Vietnamese who left their country as boat people to find freedom around the world. One fifth of them died on the high seas. Thousands of Vietnamese boat people were attacked and raped by Thai fishermen in the Gulf of Thailand.

The Wave of the Boat People

The Vietnamese Communists invaded South Vietnam in April 30, 1975. Right after the fall of Saigon, over 130,000 Vietnamese people fled their country to find freedom.[99] Each year thereafter, hundreds of thousands of Vietnamese fled out of their country by any means, in whatever boats they could find, such as fishing boats, riverboats, and sampans.[100] The shortest destination was Thailand, a neighbor and a former ally of South Vietnam.

---

[99] Vu Thuy Hoang, "Sea Crossing" (Springfield, Virginia: Vietnam Books, Inc., 1982), p. 23.

[100] Sampans: the small river boats.

In South Vietnam, before April 1975, there were over 15,000 fishing boats and over 50,000 riverboats, which were over 30 feet in length. Since the high percentage of illicit escapes, from 1975 through 1978, the riverboats, which were longer than 30 feet in length, were hard to find in the late 70's. Therefore, the boat people used the old ones and built up them as high as they could.

Escaping by boat is an adventure.[101] But every adventure has a high price: gold, blood, tears, dread, and disaster.[102] 'Boat People' is a new term, synonymous with sorrow and piteousness.[103]

The "Export of Vietnamese Boat People"

Collecting of Gold
The unofficial organization by the Vietnamese Communists was established to control the Vietnamese boat people after a high number of people fled the country in 1977.[104] The Communists took the fishing boats from the fishermen who had left them behind. These fishing boats now belonged to the new government. Each person who wanted to get out the country must pay the organization 8 to 12 ounces of gold.

The estimation of the collection of gold from 1978 to 1980 was over ten tons. Parts of this collection were sent to Hanoi to the Politburo of the Communist Party. The rest were in hands of the members of the organization. According to a book entitled "Exodus Vietnam," the Vietnamese Communists collected about three billion dollars in total through the "export of Vietnamese boat people."[105]

---

[101] Vu Thuy Hoang, "Sea Crossing" (Springfield, Virginia: Vietnam Books, Inc., 1982), p. 77.
[102] Cao The Dung, "Exodus Vietnam" (Laguna Niguel, California: Dan Tam, 1990), p. 14.
[103] IBID, p. 47.
[104] IBID, p. 25.
[105] IBID, p. 17.

Pushing the Boat People on the high seas
The Communists put as many people as possible into a fishing boat. They did not care for these boat people who would live or die on the high seas. What they cared about was how much gold they could get from these people.

The Enjoyment of Gold
During the Vietnam War, the high rank officers of the Hanoi Communists did not have any ounces of gold. They did not have their own property either. Their property belonged to the government. After the invasion of the South Vietnam, all politburo officials suddenly became rich. How? They took people's properties such as houses, land, gold, automobile, and hard currency, etc.

Now, as rich people, they enjoyed their new properties. They built new houses, bought new cars, and sent their children overseas for their education.

The Typhoon on the South China Sea

The Thai Fishing Fleet
There were about 50,000 fishing boats in the Thai fishing fleet.[106] This massive fleet allowed anonymity to the Thai pirates. Hundreds of islands on the Gulf of Thailand also provided the hiding places for the pirates. Some Thai fishing vessels were armed and equipped with hammers, screwdrivers, and pliers. These vessels were much faster than the Royal Thai Navy's patrol craft or marine police. Therefore, the Thai government's anti-piracy efforts could not go in affect.

The most important factor that permitted piracy to flourish is the lawlessness of southern Thailand. This area was semi-independent from control of the central government in Bangkok. Therefore, piracy had a firm niche, and the international laws against that activity seem almost irrelevant.

---

[106] "Vietnamese Boat People: Pirates' Vulnerable Prey," Committee for Refugees (February 1984), p. 4 & p. 5.

(Source: boatpeople75.tripod.com)

The Pirates' Victims

The first victims occurred as early as the first boat people arrived in the Gulf of Thailand in 1975. In these early times, the Thai fishermen took gold and hard currency from the boat people. During the increased influx of boat people, the Thai pirates attacked the victims, took gold and hard currency, and raped women and young girls.

According to The U.S. Committee For Refugees, "*In 1981, 77 percent of the boats which left Vietnam and eventually landed in Thailand were attacked. In 1982 and 1983, the percentage were 65 and 56, respectively.*"[107] The pirate attacks took a variety of savage forms. The report describes as follows:

"*Hundreds of victims have died, having been shot, knifed, beaten, or rammed; some have committed suicide under duress. If victims survive the first attack, a second is virtually certain: the average number of attacks per boat has almost consistently exceeded two since 1981 and has reached over three in some time periods. Children have told of being beaten or terrorized by pirates wielding hammers and knives. They have watched as their mothers were raped or abducted. Girls as young as six years of age have been sexually assaulted.*"[108]

The report continues:

---

[107] IBID, p. 5.
[108] IBID, p. 5.

"In 1982, almost 53 percent of the boats were subject to rape or abduction attacks. Between January and November 1983, abductions and rapes were occurring at almost the same rate in the preceding year. The figures are thought to understate the extent of the crimes, as they are based solely on accounts of boat people known to United Nations High Commissioner for Refugees, and many are reluctant to report rapes to outsiders. The statistics also do not reflect that women are often assaulted repeatedly or that abductees are usually also rape victims."[109] (See the statistics in the table below.)

Pirate Attacks on Boat People Arriving in Thailand[110]
1981-1983

Description	1981	1982	1983*
No. of Persons Arrived	15,095	5,913	3,171
No. of Deaths from Attack**	571	155	43
No. of Abductees***	243	157	89
(No. Traced)	(78)	(92)	(35)
No. of Rape Victims***	599	179	85
No. of Persons Missing	N/A.	443	153
No. of Boats Arrived	455	218	138
No. of Boats Attacked	352	141	77
(Percent)	(77%)	(65%)	(56%)
No. of Attacks	1,149	381	173
Average No. of Attacks Per Attacked Boat	3.2	2.7	2.3

Source: UN High Commissioner for Refugees
Note: These statistics are based solely upon reports by boat people.
*   Through November 1983.
**   Includes only piracy-related deaths, e.g. Shooting, knifing, beating, ramming, and suicide under duress.
      Accidental deaths or deaths due to sickness or starvation are not included.
***   Abductees are generally, but not always, also rape victims. Abduction and rape figures here are mutually exclusive. A person who is both an abductee and a rape victim is counted only as an abductee.

---

[109]   IBID, p. 6.
[110]   IBID, p. 6.

I was hurt by the news. One poem of mine was written for a young victim of Ko Kra Island (See "Your Youth, Little Sister", Lament of The Boat People, Lulu.com, 2008, pp. 45-46).

(Source: boatpeople75.tripod.com)

Ko Kra Island

Ko Kra Island is in the Gulf of Thailand. This island was a good place for Thai pirates to attack the boat people. They raped, beaten, rammed, and left them to die by starvation. One friend of mine, a Vietnamese novelist, was a victim of Ko Kra island. After evacuating to a refugee camp, he and other two reporters wrote a "white paper" and sent it to the Vietnamese newspapers and magazines around the world.

After the news spread out over the world, I wrote a poem to dedicate the Ko Kra Island's victims. This poem was printed in many Vietnamese magazines and newspapers around the world. It was translated into English and was published in the *"War and Exile,"* a Vietnamese Anthology, by Vietnamese PEN Abroad/East Coast U.S.A., 1987 (pp. 218-219).

According to the two Vietnamese writers, who wrote of their experience on the Ko Kra island, *"Pirates attacked one man (from the Vietnamese boat people) with hammers, screwdrivers, and pliers to remove his gold teeth. One woman washed ashore from a refugee boat attacked by other pirates was raped as she reached land. Others became 'wives' of pirates to avoid being passed from one man to another."*[111]

---

[111] Nhat Tien, Duong Phuc, and Vu Thanh Thuy, "Pirates on the Gulf of Siam"

In an article "Vietnam Couple Describe 20 Day Ordeal," the two writers reported: *"There was a girl, 12 years old, who hid in a crevice in the side of a wooden mountain... terrified of every sound she heard. After suffering thus for 15 days, she could not help but leave her hiding place, only to be raped on the spot by four pirates."[112]*

The report continued, *"Many women left their families and tried to hide, crawling under brush or clinging to mountainsides. Some refused to leave the brush even after pirates set fire to it and were badly burned. Vietnamese men who refused to reveal the hiding places were beaten with hammers and hanged."[113]*

From October 29 to November 18, 1979, the report said, the Thai pirates' actions on 157 boat people as follows:

1. Threw 17 people into the sea. All of them had died.
2. Raped continuously women and young girls, day and night, during a 21-day period.
3. Set fire to the hiding places to find women.
4. Treated badly and tortured refugee men to death.
5. Used hammers, screwdrivers, and pliers to remove the gold teeth of refugees.[114]

(Source: boatpeople75.tripod.com)

(San Diego, California: Boat People S.O.S. Committee), p. 110.

[112] IBID, p. 110.
[113] IBID, p. 110.
[114] IBID, p. 10.

The Unwilling Prostitutes

According to UNHCR report, *"Clearly, young girls and women are victimized in disproportionate measure. Over a period of almost three years ending in November 1983, most of the nearly 500 persons reported as kidnapped were female. Of that number, fewer than half has been found: abductees are often simply thrown overboard. Some women are sold into prostitution by their captors."*[115]

The Boat People's defense

(Source: boatpeople75.tripod.com)

The U. S. Committee for Refugees' report described how the Vietnamese boat people defended themselves as follows:
"The boat people put up little resistance to the attacks, although some survivors have said they tried to defend themselves. Nearly all travel unarmed, as it has been difficult to obtain unauthorized weapons in Vietnam since 1975, especially for those considered suspect by the (Communists) government."

"In any event, the boat people believe that weapons would probably be useless as a defense against pirates. Often, violent attacks occur after the voyagers have been at sea for many days and are exhausted from their exposure to the elements and their meager rations. Further, there is a widely held belief that resistance will mean death for children or for everyone aboard in retribution. Also, boat people know that pirates can communicate by radio with confederates and bring reinforcements."[116]

---

[115] "Vietnamese Boat People: Pirates' Vulnerable Prey," Committee for Refugees (February 1984), p. 5.

[116] IBID, p. 7.

The Vietnamese Boat People's Mental Health

The Vietnamese boat people's mental health is a big concern. According to the United Nations High Commissioner for Refugees, *"Aside from the physiological problems caused by rape, the women experience long-lasting psychological and emotional problems. These include depression and anxiety over possible pregnancy, loss of esteem by family and friends, and what their experiences will mean for their chances of a happy marriage."*[117]

They either were rescued to the refugee camps in southern Thailand, *"there was no counseling for rape victims, and abortions are not available. Even in the camp, women remain vulnerable: security is weak and allegedly has been violated."*[118]

The activity of the Thai pirates' in the Gulf of Thailand is a terrible memory for the Vietnamese boat people. It is a wound, a bloodstain, and a vestige in the heart of the boat people.

(Germantown, September 1998)

(Source: boatpeople75.tripod.com)

---

[117] IBID, p. 6.
[118] IBID, p. 7.

My Motherland

She is thin and tall. Her head is facing toward the North and her foot is standing on the South. Her right hand is touching the Pacific Ocean and her left hand is reaching her neighbors, Laos and Cambodia. She is almost five thousand years old. Her name is Vietnam. I call her "Motherland."

I was born in the South of Vietnam. She loved me and taught me her native language of Vietnamese. I called it the Vietnamese language. She named me "Young Patriot." I love her very much.

During the French invasion of Vietnam, I was too young to understand, but I learned how to take care of my motherland. She hated the war but she must fight for her independence. Her body was weak but her mind was too strong. She defeated the French troops in 1954 in the North. The independence was in her hand, but she could not hold on for long.

On July 20th, 1954, the Vietnamese Communists took over the North right after the Paris Peace Agreement. Over one million people in the North escaped to the South to find freedom. At the same time, the people in the South established a free government in Saigon and Saigon became its capital. It was called the South Vietnam or the Republic of Vietnam. Mr. Ngo Dinh Diem became Prime Minister of the South Vietnamese government. The South Vietnamese people selected him as a president of the South Vietnam in 1955.

During his presidency, from 1955 to 1963, Mr. Diem tried to prevent the growth of Communists in the South. The United States gave South Vietnam the military aid to prevent the Communists.

With the strong support from the Soviet Union and China, North Vietnam sent Communist troops into the South via Ho Chi Minh Trail in Laos and Cambodia. The United States government became heavily involved with military in South Vietnam with the hope that it would prevent the Vietnamese Communists at the 17th Parallel. On the other hand, President Richard Nixon normalized his relationship with China in hope to separate the two super powers – China and Soviet Union – so the United States could defeat the North Vietnam and achieve its goal.

In 1963, the United States government wanted to send more troops into South Vietnam but President Diem did not agree. That disagreement caused the coup d'etat in 1963 with the death of President Diem and his young brother, Ngo Dinh Nhu.

In 1965, the United States government sent hundreds of thousands of GI's to South Vietnam to fight directly with Communists. The Vietnam War began to escalate heavily.

As a young compatriot, I had no choice but to fight in the armed forces. I volunteered to join the Vietnamese Navy. I did not fight directly with Communists, except the Tet Offensive in 1968. I was in the Vietnamese Navy Headquarters on the eve of the New Year. Thirteen Communists were killed that night, just outside the Vietnamese Navy Headquarters.

During the Tet Offensive, the Hanoi Communists killed thousands of civilians. There were over ten thousand casualties and people missing. Several cities in the South were badly damaged. In exchange, thousands of Communists were killed, injured or captured.

After the Tet Offensive, Hanoi agreed to go to Paris for a peace talk with the United States. In 1972, Hanoi signed the Paris Peace Agreement. In the same time, Hanoi sent more troops to the South.

In early April 1975, the war was strong and terrible. The Communists took control over some places in the Central and the Highlands. Finally, the Hanoi Communists invaded the South Vietnam in April 30, 1975.

After the surrender of President Duong Van Minh, a two-day president, South Vietnam's Armed Forces had almost disintegrated. I had no means to flee the country. In the evening of that day, a friend of mine, a Vietnamese Navy officer, gave me a riverboat to get out the country. I left everything behind me: my motherland, my parents, and my family.

During over 22 years in exile, I try to fight for my motherland. I hope I will bring freedom back to Vietnam. In one of my poems, *One Day Will Come*, I wrote:

> *"I wish I could return home some day,*
> *We will enjoy freedom that we pray."* [119]

---

[119]   Vinh Liem, "Without Beginning Without End" (Lulu.com, 2008), pp. 1-2.

My motherland is still alive but her body is ill. The Communist regime sold some of her parts to China, such as Paracel Islands and Spratly Islands. The Communist leaders and their officials are very rich, but Vietnamese people are very poor. Under the Communist regime, my motherland is one of the poorest countries.

(Germantown, 02-23-1998)

Prophet Huynh Phu So
(1919 – 1947)

"I ACCEPT TO SUFFER IN YOUR PLACE," said Prophet Huynh Phu So,
when French Colonialists arrested Him.

Prophet HUYNH PHU SO, the founder of Hoa-Hao Buddhism, was
born in 1919 in Hoa-Hao village, Chau Doc province, South
Western of Vietnam. He was the eldest son of The Venerable Huynh
Cong Bo and Le Thi Nham.

In May 18, 1939 (lunar month, the year of the Hare), Prophet Huynh
Phu So founded Hoa-Hao Buddhism. Since then, Hoa-Hao
Buddhism has grown rapidly into a major religion. Its influence has
spread over the Mekong River Delta which is the Western part of
South Vietnam, including many provinces and city, such as: Chau
Doc, An Giang, Sadec, Kien Phong, Vinh Long, Phong Dinh,
Chuong Thien, Kien Giang, Ba Xuyen, Bac Lieu, An Xuyen, Dinh
Tuong, Long An, Kien Hoa, Kien Tuong, Gia Dinh and Saigon.
Prophet Huynh achieved His first conversions by reputedly curing
incurable diseases with simple means, such as pure water and green
leaves.

In His salvation mission, Prophet Huynh preached thousands of times to large audiences. His works were published in six Books of Oracle, as well as hundreds of sublime poems, essays and folk litanies. His writings, without any draft, presented popular overtones but proved extremely soul stirring and impressive.

Prophet Huynh gave to the world a great number of oracles. He foretold the expansion of World War II as well as the spread of sufferings, exhorted mankind to renounce vice and come back to virtue. He asked His believers to observe the Four Debts of Gratitude and improve oneself through contemplation so as to become "good individual in the society and progress on the path of deliverance."

Within a year He became very popular and attracted million believers, so the French colonial authorities began to worry about the extraordinary expansion of His religious movement. Thus they placed Him under house arrest at Nhon Nghia village, Can Tho province. At Nhon Nghia He became more popular and adored than ever before. Therefore, the French authorities placed Him under administrative surveillance at Cho Quan Hospital (as known as a mental hospital) in Cho Lon and later they transferred Him to Bac Lieu province. When Japanese troops occupied Vietnam in early 1945, they forced the French authorities to transfer Prophet Huynh to their Kempeitai Headquarters in Saigon.

Right after the defeat of Japan (August 1945), Prophet Huynh assumed the responsibility of protecting the nation and saving His countrymen by founding and participating many fronts, associations, movements, and political party (see His religion and political activities on the next page).

In April 16, 1947, Vietnamese Communists trapped Him in an ambush (outside a conference room) at Doc Vang village, in the Plain of Reeds. Since then, nobody hears from Him yet, but His followers firmly believe that He could not be harmed; and they are waiting for the day He will return when His glorious mission had been completed.

Religion and Political Activities:
- Honorary Adviser of Vietnam Patriot Party / Việt Nam Ái Quốc Đảng (2/1945)
- Founder of Movement for Vietnam Independence / Việt Nam Độc Lập Vận Động Hội (3/1945)
- Founder of Union of Vietnam Buddhist Associations / Việt Nam Phật Giáo Liên Hiệp Hội (4/1945)
- Co-founder of National Unified Front / Mặt Trận Thống Nhứt Quốc Gia (1945)
- Co-founder of Front for National Union / Mặt Trận Liên Hiệp Quốc Gia (1946)
- Co-founder of Association for Vietnamese Peoples Union / Hội Liên Hiệp Quốc Dân Việt Nam (1946)
- Member of Administrative Committee of South Vietnam / Ủy Ban Hành Chánh Nam Bộ as a Special Commissioner (2/1946)
- Founder of Vietnamese Democratic Socialist Party / Đảng Việt Nam Dân Chủ Xã Hội aka Việt Nam Dân Xã Đảng (September 21, 1946)

Characteristics of Hoa-Hao Buddhism

Prophet Huynh Phu So created Hoa-Hao Buddhism in 1939. Until April 1975, Hoa-Hao Buddhism was one of the four most important religions in Vietnam. With a mass of over two million faithful closely united in their faith, Hoa-Hao Buddhism became an influential force in South Vietnam.[120] This force was so well organized that it not only survived but also continues to develop through severe trials and hardships.

Hoa-Hao Buddhism is not an entirely new religion in Vietnam. In fact, it is a fundamental Buddhist religion associated with two other greatest and oldest doctrines of oriental philosophy (Confucianism and Taoism) whose influences have been deep in the hearts of the Vietnamese people for centuries.

With the extreme richness of its doctrine, Hoa-Hao Buddhism has been very influential within the Vietnamese Churches, which, along with other Buddhist Churches in the world, is guiding mankind to a new society, to new spiritual values, and to the deliverance of mankind.

---

[120] "A Brief Description of Hoa-Hao Buddhism," Hoa-Hao Buddhist Church, Overseas Office (1983), p. 7.

Hoa-Hao Buddhism has four special characteristics: Buddhism for the peasants, the practice of Buddhism at home, "study Buddhism to improve yourselves," and the modernization of the methods of self-improvement.

Buddhism for the Peasants

The first characteristic of Hoa-Hao Buddhism is Buddhism for the peasants. The fact is that, from Buu-Son Ky-Huong to Hoa-Hao, it has always been Buddhism for the peasants.

During his lifetime, Master Buddha of Tay-An, who founded Buu-Son Ky-Huong Buddhism, used to preach Buddhism and at the same time encouraged agriculture. His slogan: *"Practicing Buddhism while cultivating your land."*

In continuing the tradition of Buu-Son Ky-Huong Buddhism, Prophet Huynh Phu So also encouraged agriculture. This is the reason why He chose the most fertile part of Vietnam to begin His evangelical mission, and why the majority of the Hoa-Hao faithful are farmers.

In the human and social fields, it is known that the farmers, by their pure and simple nature, can practice Buddhism most correctly.

To understand why this tradition is very important, we must review the three basic elements: the physical background, the origin, and the Hoa-Hao followers.

Physical background

In 1939, Prophet Huynh Phu So founded Hoa-Hao Buddhism. Since then, it has grown rapidly into a major religion. Its influence spreads over the Mekong River Delta. It is called Western Buddhism. The highly fertile area of the Mekong Delta plays a very important part in the agricultural economy of Vietnam. Most of the rice exports come from here. It is known as the Rice basket of Vietnam. The Western Area covers an area of 18,850 square kilometers of arable land producing 3,000,000 tons of rice per year.

With total area of 173,260 square kilometers, South Vietnam has about 30,000 square kilometers under cultivation. The Western Area, where Hoa-Hao Buddhism was founded, occupies 60 percent of the total cultivable land of the country.

Origin

The mountains of the Western area have been the source of many unexplainable mysteries. The most famous of these are the Sacred Mountains of That Son, on the border of Chau-Doc province and Cambodia.

Since 1849, a living Buddha reverently known as Master Buddha of Tay-An made his first appearance on the Sacred Mountains of That Son and began his salvation mission by creating Buu-Son Ky-Huong Buddhism. About 90 years later, exactly in 1939, also near That-Son Mountains, another living Buddha, Prophet Huynh Phu So, continued the tradition of Buu-Son Ky-Huong and founded Hoa-Hao Buddhism. Therefore, although Hoa-Hao Buddhism was founded in 1939, it is a continuation of the Buu-Son Ky-Huong established in 1849. Thus its existence is over a century old.

Both Master Buddha of Tay-An and Prophet Huynh Phu So have been revered throughout South Vietnam as two Buddhas coming into the world to save mankind from sufferings. They have also been respectfully regarded as two genuine patriots.

Hoa-Hao Followers

The total number of Hoa-Hao followers is estimated at over two million people representing more than one third the population of the Western Area, or 10 percent of the total population of South Vietnam.[121]

In such provinces as Chau-Doc, An-Giang, Kien-Phong and Sadec, Hoa-Hao Buddhists account for 90 percent of the population. In other provinces, this proportion varies from 10 to 60 percent.

The Practice of Buddhism at Home

The second characteristic is that both Hoa-Hao Buddhism and Buu-Son Ky-Huong advocate the practice of Buddhism at home. The reason was that both Master Buddha of Tay-An and Prophet Huynh Phu So shared the same view that Buddhism should not only be preached in pagodas and temples, but also be propagated largely into every family. It is a convenience for the farmers.

According to the reform, worshipping at a Hoa-Hao Buddhist home should be very simple. On the altar, there is no Buddha statue, bell or gong, but a piece of brown clothing. It symbolizes the human Harmony and the color of Buddhism. Under the Buddha's altar is the Ancestral altar for the cult of Ancestors. In front of the house is set up a Heaven's altar to enable communication with the universe (sky and earth), the Four Sky Directions, and the Ten Buddhist Directions.

"No food of any kind including fruits may be used to worship Buddha. Only fresh water, flowers and incense sticks are needed. Fresh water is to present cleanliness and flowers to purity. And incense sticks are to freshen the air." [122]

---

[121] Hinh Phuong, "Hoa Hao Buddhist Organization," Phuong Dong Magazine, No. 23 (May 1973).

[122] "A Brief Description of Hoa-Hao Buddhism," Hoa-Hao Buddhist Church, Overseas Office (1983), p. 12.

Hoa-Hao followers must worship Buddha at least twice a day: in the morning and in the evening. On the 1st and 15th of each lunar month and on Buddha's Holy days, they have to go to Hoa-Hao Preaching Halls or pagodas to pray and listen to sermons. Prayers are to be in a low voice while no bells or gongs may be used.

When the time of worship comes, if they are away from home, they turn Westwards to pray to Buddha. They should also encourage others to pray silently in their heart wherever they may be.

At each hamlet, there is at least one Preaching Hall that equipped with the loud speakers. Every day, at special hours, a Preacher would come there to read prayers or to give sermons to the audiences.

Hoa-Hao Buddhist Preaching Halls are small Pagodas. They are used for the unique purpose of preaching. As they do not have residential quarters, they are much smaller than pagodas or temples, because Hoa-Hao Buddhism puts more emphasis on the practice of Buddhism at home.

Over two million of Hoa-Hao followers practicing Buddhism at home not only do their best to improve themselves physically and spiritually, but they also contribute greatly to the development of the agricultural economy of their country.

"Study Buddhism to Improve Yourselves"

The guideline of Hoa-Hao Buddhism Doctrine is *"Study Buddhism to improve yourselves."* This means that we must observe the genuine teachings of Buddha to make ourselves better in order to fulfill our duty in our present life, and to be able to reach the Buddhist Paradise to freeing ourselves from the law of Metempsychosis.

In practicing Buddhism for self-improvement, a Hoa-Hao Buddhist must first of all do his or her best to comply with the Four Debts of Gratitude:

Thankfulness to our Ancestors and Parents

According to Prophet Huynh Phu So's Teachings, *"We were born with a body to be active from our childhood to manhood with a given wisdom and knowledge."* Our parents have suffered during our childhood years. Remember that our ancestors gave birth to our parents, therefore, we must be as grateful to our ancestors as we are towards our parents.

To show our gratitude towards our ancestors, we cannot do anything that is wicked or shameful to our family's name. If our ancestors, for example, had done anything wrong and left a legacy of sufferings to their decedents, we should dedicate ourselves to act in compliance with the moral principles to restore our ancestors' honor.

To show our gratitude to our parents, we must obey the right lessons they teach us and must not annoy them. If our parents did anything wrong or acted against moral laws, we should do our best to advise and prevent them from doing so. We should also support them and keep them from hunger and sickness. To please our parents, we should bring accord among our brothers and sisters and happiness to our family. We always pray for our parents to enjoy happiness and longevity. When they die, we pray for their soul to be freed from sufferings in the Buddhist Kingdom. [123]

(Photo: R. Johan O Alt - Flickr)

---

[123] "Biography and Teachings of Prophet Huynh-Phu-So," Hoa-Hao Buddhist Church, Overseas Office (1983), pp. 13-14.

Thankfulness to our Country

We always owe our living to our native land. If we want our life to be happy and our race to survive, while enjoying our land and its produce, we have a duty to defend our country; therefore, we must contribute to the safeguarding of our fatherland. Whenever there is a foreign invasion, we must liberate it. In case we have no talent to assume responsibilities or no opportunity to help our country, we must avoid wrong doings that may hurt our country. We should never help the enemy to harm our fatherland. [124]

Thankfulness to the Three Treasures: Buddha, Buddhist Law, and Sangha

According to Prophet Huynh Phu So, man is born and brought up thanks to his ancestors and parents. He owes his existence to his country. That is the physical aspect of life. In the spiritual field, man needs the help of Buddha, the Teachings of Buddhism, and the Priests to open his mind.

Buddha is the most flawless and most perfect creature. General speaking, Buddha is infinitely altruistic and determined to save living creatures from misfortune and suffering. That is why He bequeathed His Teachings to the Priests so as to disseminate them through the world. Remember that, the Priests are none but Buddha's great disciples.

As Buddha always guides and saves human beings from bewilderment and suffering, we must respect Him. We believe and have confidence in His world-salvation work. Furthermore, we must comply with His Teachings that the Priests conveyed to us. We must also respect and venerate Buddha. We act in compliance with His Teachings and have cultivated and strengthened our religion so as to expand it. This act is building a castle of peerless and unparalleled virtue bequeathed to posterity.

---

[124] IBID, p. 14.

Our duty is to follow our ancestors' highest virtues. We have a clear mind to reach the path of deliverance and help those who fall into misfortune. We must also especially continue to cultivate and spread Compassion and Fraternity everywhere among human beings. [125]

Thankfulness to our fellow-countrymen and to mankind

Since our birth, we depend on people around us. As we grow up, our dependency on them grows. We need their grains to live on, their clothes to keep ourselves warm, and their houses as shelters against weather adversities. We always enjoy happiness and share misfortune with them.

According to Prophet Huynh Phu So, they and we are of the same culture and tradition, history, and language. Together we form our nation. We call them our fellow-countrymen. Our fellow-countrymen and we are of the same root. We have the same illustrious and heroic history. We must help each other in distress. We have also the same task of building a bright future for our country. Our fellow-countrymen and we have a close relationship. We are indivisible and undetectable. We never would be there without our fellow-countrymen or vice-versa. We must, therefore, do our best to help and show them in some way our gratitude for their assistance.

(Photo: Hoang Viet - Flickr)

---

[125] IBID, pp. 14-15.

Besides our fellow-countrymen, there are other peoples in the world who are working hard to supply us with necessities. They are the human race those who live with us on this earth. We must be grateful to them. We must think of them as we do of ourselves and of our own compatriots. Moreover, Buddha's mercy and compassion are very wide and deep. In his view, they are boundless. They have no discrimination of race and social status. They are bestowed upon all living creatures. There is, therefore, no valid reason for us to do harm to other people only for our own sake or that of our fellow countrymen. On the contrary, we should have a spirit of concord and indulgence towards them. We should make it our duty to help them in case of distress.

For the priests who have taken refuge in Buddhism, they should thank their donators who supply them with daily needs because they depend on them for their rice, clothes, and medicine. In brief, they are entirely dependent on the kindness of these people. They are deeply indebted to everyone. In order to show their gratitude, they should guide mankind in the search for Truth. [126]

The Modernization of the Methods of Self-improvement

The fourth characteristic of Hoa-Hao Buddhism is the modernization of the methods of self-improvement by discarding all futile rites and superstitious practices. This is made to show the essence of Buddhism in accordance with genuine Buddha's teachings.

Here are some modifications advocated by Hoa-Hao Buddhism:

Pagodas

---

[126] IBID, pp. 15-16.

Neither pagodas nor statues should be built besides the existing ones. Hoa-Hao Buddhist followers reserve their money to come to the assistance of the poor and the needy. That is a really beneficial act unlike building a large pagoda or casting the tall and expensive statues.

Services

Hoa-Hao Buddhism followers do not require the services of sorcerers, magicians, astrologers, and fortune-tellers. They do not offer food as offerings to Buddha because they believe that Buddha would never accept such bribery. They do also not use flags, banners or streamers. They do not burn votive paper because this is a waste of money.

Marriage

Hoa-Hao Buddhist followers do not compel their children to marry the one they do not like or love. They do not demand matrimonial deposit money from the groom or organize big wedding parties, because this will result in impoverishing themselves.

Funerals

Hoa-Hao Buddhist Followers do not cry or conduct expensive funerals; instead they pray quietly for the deliverance of the deceased's soul.

***

In short, the reform advocated by Hoa-Hao Buddhism is aimed at bringing us back to the original teachings of Buddha. He taught: *"Our belief must come from our heart."* It is only a matter of heart and not a matter of rite and ceremony.

(Germantown, August 21, 1998)

VINH LIEM'S WORKS OF ART AND TECHNICAL

BOOKS PUBLISHED IN VIETNAM

BOOK OF POEMS
1. *'Tho Vinh Liem'* (Vinh Liem's Poems) written in Vietnamese, published in 1974

BOOKS READY FOR PUBLICATION IN VIETNAM
ALL WORKS FELL INTO COMMUNIST HANDS AND WERE DESTROYED

A. BOOKS OF POEMS (1964-1975) written in Vietnamese
1. *'Loi Tu Tinh Cua Bien'* (The Ocean's Whispering)
2. *'Tu Thu'* (Confession)
3. *'Que Huong Trong Trai Tim Nguoi'* (The Native Land In One's Heart)
4. *'Coi Doi Hiu Quanh'* (The Deserted Life)
5. *'Cat Vang'* (The Yellow Sands)

B. COLLECTIONS OF SHORT STORIES (1964-1975) written in Vietnamese
1. *'Mua Xuan Cua Nang'* (The Spring of Her Life)
2. *'Loi Thoat'* (The Way Out)
3. *'Que Nha'* (Fatherland)

C. NOVEL (1970-1975) written in Vietnamese
1. *'Go Cua Tinh Yeu'* (The First Love)

BOOKS WERE PUBLISHED IN THE UNITED STATES

A. BOOKS OF POEMS
1. *'Ti Nan Truong Ca,'* *Tap I* (The Refugee's Lasting Chantey), Vol. I, Vietnamese, published in 1980
2. *'Bi Ca Nguoi Vuot Bien'* (Lament of The Boat People), Vietnamese, published in 1980
3. *'Ti Nan Truong Ca,'* *Tap II* (The Refugee's Lasting Chantey), Vol. II, Vietnamese, published in 1982

4. *'Without Beginning Without End'*, poetry, English, published in 2008.
5. *'Lament of The Boat People'*, Poetry & Essays, English & Vietnamese, published in 2008

B. COLLECTION OF SHORT STORIES
1. *'Ga Ti Nan'* (The Refugee Guy), a collection of short stories, written in Vietnamese, published in 1986

BOOKS READY FOR PUBLICATION

A. BOOKS OF POEMS (in Vietnamese)
1. *'Ti Nan Truong Ca,' Tap III* (The Refugee's Lasting Chantey), Vol. III.
2. *'Ti Nan Truong Ca,' Tap IV* (The Refugee's Lasting Chantey), Vol. IV.
3. *'Ti Nan Truong Ca,' Tap V* (The Refugee's Lasting Chantey), Vol. V.
4. *'Ti Nan Truong Ca,' Tap VI* (The Refugee's Lasting Chantey), Vol. VI.
5. *'Ti Nan Truong Ca,' Tap VII* (The Refugee's Lasting Chantey), Vol. VII.
6. *'Huong Dong Noi'* (Fragrance).
7. *'Thang Hoa'* (Sublimation).
8. *'Con Vuong To Long'* (Ties of Affection).

B. COLLECTIONS OF SHORT STORIES (in Vietnamese)
1. *'Hanh Phuc Phia Ben Kia'* (Motherland's Happiness)
2. *'Ngay Xuan Chua Du Am'* (The Springtime Without Happiness)
3. *'Hoi Huong'* (Repatriation)

C. MUSIC/SONGS/THEATER (in Vietnamese)
1. *'Thuyen Tinh'* (Boat of Love), collection of songs
2. *'Nhat Dinh Thang'* (Decided Victory*),* collection of songs
3. *'Co Nhac Viet Nam'* (Vietnamese Renovated Theater and Traditional Music)

D. LITERATURE (in Vietnamese)
1. *'Vuon Hoa Van Hoc'* (Garden of Literature – Vietnamese Writers Overseas: Works and Authors)
2. *'Tha Huong Van Tap'* (Confidences on the foreign country)
3. *'Huong Sac Trong Vuon Tho'* (Fragrance in the Poetry Corner)

E. RELIGION (in Vietnamese)
1. *'Nep Song Hoa-Hao'* (Hoa-Hao Buddhism's Life)

F. POLITICS (in Vietnamese)
1. *'The Luc Nao?'* (What's Influence?)
2. *'Tuyen Tap Can Bo'* (Political Cadre's Handbook)

G. COLLECTIONS OF ESSAYS (in Vietnamese)
1. *'Chuyen Ben Le'* (The Sideline's Stories)
2. *'Nguoc Gio'* (Up The Wind) – an idle talk
3. *'Minh Oi!'* (My Dear!) – comic stories

H. BUSINESS, ECONOMICS, & FINANCE (in English)
1. *'Loan Officer's Handbook'*
2. *'Mortgage Processor's Handbook'*
3. *'Dictionary of Real Estate and Mortgage'*
4. *'New Vietnam, Great Opportunities'*
5. *'Real Estate and Mortgage Markets in Vietnam'*

Contact Information:
Email: vinhliem9@hotmail.com
Home Page: http://vinhliem.tripod.com
1 Applegrath Court, Germantown, MD 20876-5613 (USA)

$15.95 USA / $20.50 CAN